NORTH AYRSHIRE
06858015

D0682184

First published in Great Britain in 2014 by Comma Press.
www.commapress.co.uk

The section from the professor's journal in 'The Taxidermist's Daughter' is an edited quotation from an archival source held in manuscript at the National Library of Wales: *The Natural History Diary of Dr J. H. Salter*, Vols. 6 and 7, 1898 and 1900, NLW MS 14436B and NLW MS 14437B. It should however be noted that this story is a work of fiction.

A CIP catalogue record of this book is available from the British Library.

ISBN-13 978-1905583676
ISBN-10 1905583672

The publisher gratefully acknowledges the assistance of Literature Northwest and Arts Council England across all its projects.

Set in Bembo 11/13 by David Eckersall.
Printed and bound in England by Berforts Information Press.

2014

THE BBC NATIONAL SHORT STORY AWARD

Contents

Introduction

IT HAS BEEN quite a year for short fiction. When Alice Munro was awarded the Nobel Prize for literature in October 2013, it was hailed as a watershed moment. For the first time ever, literature's top prize was awarded to, in the words of Jonathan Franzen a '*pure* short story' writer. What's more, a few months earlier Lydia Davis, another master teller of the shortest of short tales (some of her stories are two lines long), received The Man Booker International Prize. This year, the Independent Foreign Fiction Prize was won by a short story collection for the first time – Hassan Blasim's *The Iraqi Christ* – and finally, the newest literary accolade on the block, the UK's inaugural Folio Prize was also won, not by a novel but a collection of short stories from American author George Saunders.

So what's going on? The last 100 years have given us some remarkable collections of short fiction: Raymond Carver, John Cheever, Jean Rhys to name only a few. I have been privileged to meet many of them, from Rhys to Jorge Luis Borges, and Doris Lessing to William Trevor. Indeed, one of the first films I made for the BBC hand-in-glove with my colleague Nigel Williams, was a collaboration with Trevor – or let's call it a collusion. A short film about a short story writer, filmed by two apprentice filmmakers and penned by a master of his craft.

Yet the current buzz around the form feels unprecedented. Even as I write, one of this country's most admired novelists, David Mitchell, is publishing his latest work – yes a short story, on Twitter. That's 280 Tweets at a 140 characters or less. Until recently considered the enemy of literature, could it be that the web is becoming an enabler of a certain kind of storytelling? There's no escaping the fact that the short narrative has emerged from the shadows to take centre stage and bask in the spotlight.

Happily, the enthusiasm of writers both established and emerging is very much in evidence in this, the ninth BBC National Short Story Award in partnership with Booktrust. That much is apparent from the number of entries, over 550, and in the quality and diversity of the work submitted. It has been a pleasure and a challenge to serve as this year's Chair. With the standard so high, whittling down a sifted selection of 64 to five shortlisted stories has been no mean feat and I would like to thank this year's judges for their dedication, their wisdom… and their patience. My gratitude then to: Adam Foulds, poet and novelist, shortlisted for the Man Booker Prize in 2009 for his novel *The Quickening Maze*; author, illustrator and performer Laura Dockrill, a regular presence on BBC radio, whose most recent book *Darcy Burdock* was shortlisted for the Waterstones Children's Book Prize; Philip Gwyn Jones, a Trustee of the Royal Literary Fund and Editor-at-Large at Scribe Publications; and finally Di Speirs, BBC Radio's Editor of Books, a mainstay of this award from the very beginning – who, as ever, will be presiding over the broadcast of the finalists' stories on Radio 4.

One of the pleasures reading a great short story affords us is the invitation to dive straight into another world, a life, a moment, a character, a place and to emerge soon after with a new perspective. This is something that all the stories in our shortlist share. Actions unfold in diverse settings, with one protagonist or more. And all this can take place in the course of a single day, an afternoon, or even a lifetime.

The art of the short story writer is ignited by curiosity and underpinned by observation. James Thurber, a prolific short story writer, recalled that sometimes, when out at a party, his wife would come up to him and say: 'Dammit Thurber, stop writing.' Even away from his desk he was habitually alert, watching, searching, always aware of the infinite possibility of every moment.

In Zadie Smith's 'Miss Adele Amidst the Corsets' an ageing American performer comes face-to-face with a multitude of resentments while buying undergarments on the East Side of New

York City. It's a short explosive encounter, but one with deep reverberations. There is freedom within the short story to unpack a moment and also to explore the passage of time. In Rose Tremain's 'The American Lover' an English woman recalls the prolonged anguish of a transfiguring, disfiguring love affair. It's an intensely moving story of a life lost to love.

In 'Kilifi Creek' Lionel Shriver takes as her subject a young gap year traveller's brief encounter with mortality, which shapes her life. It's wry, witty and understated, a masterly meditation on how we react to what life might have in store for us.

A defining characteristic shared by all five stories is their painstaking and precise use of language – not least in the words they choose to omit. In the short story, the space between words, what is left unsaid, often has great impact. This is certainly the case in Tessa Hadley's 'Bad Dreams', the shortest on our shortlist. One little girl's dream exposes the unease and isolation lurking beneath the surface of family life. Events are described but not explained. It is left for us, the readers, to surmise and speculate on the lasting consequences for mother, father and child.

The fifth and final title in our selection, Francesca Rhydderch's 'The Taxidermist's Daughter', brilliantly demonstrates how, in just a few pages, it is possible to be transported to a very different place. A young girl living with her family in post-war rural Wales is sexually awakened for the first time by the presence of an older man. But there's nothing graphic or explicit here. What's admirable about this story is its restraint. We are allowed to enter the child's world and to share her innocence.

Cormac McCarthy provocatively, though entertainingly, remarked, 'I'm not interested in writing short stories. Anything that doesn't take years of your life and drive you to suicide hardly seems worth doing.' Well, it's a point of view. But you know what, Cormac, I think it might be time for you to go with the Zeitgeist. Short really is sweet and it's never been sweeter than now.

Alan Yentob

Bad Dreams

Tessa Hadley

A CHILD WOKE up in the dark. She seemed to swim up into consciousness as if to a surface which she broke through, looking around then with her eyes open. At first the darkness was implacable, she might have arrived anywhere: all that was certain was her own self, lying on her side; the salty smell of herself and her warmth, and her knees pulled up to her skinny chest inside the cocoon of her brushed nylon nightdress. But as she stared into the darkness, familiar forms began to loom through it: the paler outline of a window, printed by the street lamp against the curtains; the horizontals on the opposite wall which were the shelves where she and her brother kept their books and toys. Beside the window she could make out a rectangle of wool cloth tacked up; her mother had appliqued onto it a sleigh and two horses and a driver cracking his whip, glueing on the pieces first and then outlining them in machine stitching, sewing star-shapes in blue thread into the falling snowflakes, lines of red stitching for the reins and the twisting whip. She knew all these details off by heart though in the dark she couldn't see them. She was here, where she always was when she woke up: in her own bedroom, in the top bunk bed – her younger brother asleep in the lower one.

Her mother and father must be in bed and asleep too. The basement flat was small enough so that if they were awake she would have heard the sewing machine or the wireless, or her father practising the trumpet or playing jazz records, or the gas geyser roaring in the bathroom. But now, deep inside the night, her parents' strong presence was in abeyance and the silence in the flat was impersonal, forbidding as a wall. The child struggled to sit up out of the tight-wound nest of sheets and blankets; she was asthmatic and feared not being able to get her breath. Cold night air struck her shoulders: it was strange to stare into the room with eyes wide open and feel the darkness only yielding the least bit, as if it pressed back against her efforts at penetrating it. Something had happened, she was sure, while she was asleep. She didn't know for a few moments what it was, but the strong dread it had left behind didn't subside as the confusion of waking subsided. Then she remembered that this thing had happened inside her sleep, while she was dreaming.

She had dreamed something horrible, and so plausible that it was vividly present as soon as she remembered it; the real world was changed by it. In the dream she had been reading her favourite book, the one she had read over and over and really had been reading earlier this same night, before her mother came in hours ago to put the light out. In fact she could feel the book's hard corner pressing now into her leg through the blankets. In the dream she had been turning its pages as usual when beyond the well-known last words she found an extra section which she had never seen before, a short paragraph set on a page by itself, headed 'Epilogue'. She was an advanced reader for her age, and knew about prologues and epilogues – though it didn't occur to her then that she was the author of her own dreams, and must have invented this epilogue herself. It seemed so completely a found thing, alien and unanticipated; coming from outside herself, against her will. Desperately she resented its invasion.

In the real book she loved, *Swallows and Amazons,* six children spent their summers in perfect freedom, sailing dinghies on a lake, acting out adventures and rivalries that were half-invented games and half-truth, pushing across the threshold of safety into a thrilling unknown. All the detail had the solidity of real life, though it wasn't her real life – she didn't have servants or boats or a lake or an absent father in the navy. *Swallows and Amazons* was more than a book to her, it was a cult; she had read all the other books in the series too, and acted out their stories with her friends at school, although they lived in a city and none of them had ever been sailing. The books' world existed in a parallel dimension to their own, not touching it except in their play. They had a *Swallows and Amazons* club, and took turns to bring in 'grub' to eat in their playtimes, 'grog' and 'pemmican'; they sewed badges, and wrote each other notes in secret code. All of them wanted to be Nancy Blackett, the strutting pirate-girl, though they would settle for Titty Walker, sensitive and watchful.

Now she seemed to see written on the dark in front of her eyes the impersonal plain print of the dream-Epilogue. *John and Roger both went on to…* it began, in its business-like voice of sanity and reality. Of course the print wasn't actually in front of her eyes, it was only a dream, and bits of the detail of what was written were elusive when she sought them; other sentences, though, were scored into her awareness as definitely as if she'd heard them read aloud. *Roger drowned at sea, at a young age.* Roger was the youngest of them all, the Ship's Boy, in whom she had only ever been mildly interested: this threw him into a terrible new prominence. *John was happily married… died of a heart attack in his forties. The Blackett sisters… long illnesses. Titty, killed in an unfortunate accident…* The litany of deaths tore jaggedly into the tissue that the book had woven, making everything lopsided and hideous. Its gloating bland language, complacently regretful, seemed to relish catching her out in her dismay, making it humiliating. Oh, didn't you know? *Susan lived to a ripe old age.* Susan was the dullest of the Swallows, tamed and sensible, in charge of cooking and housekeeping. Her *ripe* it reverently, like an incantation – though the daily business of her sewing mostly wasn't reverent but briskly pragmatic, cutting and pinning and snipping at seams with pinking shears, running the machine with her head bent close to the work, one hand always raised to the wheel to slow it, breaking threads quickly in the little clip behind the needle. The chatter of the sewing machine, racing and easing and halting and starting up again, was like a busy engine driving through their days: threads and pins scattered on the floor around where she was working and you had to be careful where you stepped. The sewing seemed her mother's whole character: mouth bristling with pins, forceful in her passionate bursts of concentration, puzzling over the scraps of cloth which she was transforming out of themselves according to inspirations from her magazine *L'Officiel de la Couture* – usually an *Officiel* from last year, because she couldn't afford to buy a newer one.

In the lounge the drip-feed oil fire, turned out of course, glugged nonetheless lugubriously once, shocking the child as she paddled her toes in the hair of the goatskin rug – the rug gleamed white, uncanny, half reverted to its animal past, yearning to the moon which hung beyond the window, balanced on top of the high wall at the back of their paved yard. All ordinary everyday things in the flat seemed withdrawn secretively behind their appearances: the silver frame of her parents' wedding photograph and the yellow brass of her father's trumpet – left in its case with the lid open, beside the music stand – shone with the same pale light. Lifting the forbidden heavy lid of the gramophone, she breathed the holy smell of the records nestled in their felt-lined compartments, then touched the pages of writing heaped up on her father's desk. His meaning, densely tangled in its black italics, seemed more accessible through her fingertips in the dark than it ever was in daylight, when its difficulty thwarted her. He was studying for his degree in the evenings after teaching in school all day – she and her brother played quietly so as not to disturb him, their mother impressed them with the importance of his work. He wrote things about a book, *Leviathan;* his ink bottle left prints of its shape on the desk's leather inlay and he stored his notes on a shelf in cardboard folders, carefully labelled – the pile of folders growing ever higher. She was struck by the melancholy of this accumulation of his efforts: she felt this pang of fear for her father sometimes, as if he was exposed and vulnerable – and yet when he wasn't working he charmed them with his jokes, pretending to be poisoned when he tasted the cakes she had made, teasing her school friends until they blushed. She never feared for her mother so painfully: her mother was capable, she was the whole world.

Each detail in the dim-lit scene seemed final, as if she couldn't make any mark on it or change it. In their absence her parents were more distinctly present to her than usual, as individuals with their own unfathomable adult preoccupations, laid down only for this interlude while they slept: she was aware of their lives running backwards from this moment, into their past which she could never enter. And this present moment too, the one fitted around her now inevitably and closely as a skin, would one day become the past: its details then would seem remarkable and poignant, and she would never be able to return inside them. Her thoughts, she recognised, were taking on the tone of ripe resignation and fatality in the dream-epilogue. *Her childhood was very happy. Her beloved parents…* Fragments hovered outside her, written on the air. *Later in life… inconsolable… soon learned… the loss of…* Violently she wanted to disrupt this world of her home, sealed in its mysterious stillness, where her bare feet made no sound on the kitchen lino or the carpets.

The chairs in the lounge, looming formidably in the dimness, seemed drawn up for a spectacle, waiting more attentively than if they were filled with people: the angular recliner built of black tubular steel with lozenges of polished wood for arms, the cone-shaped wicker basket in its round wrought iron frame, the black-painted wooden arm chair with orange cushions, the low divan covered in striped olive green cotton. The reality of these things seemed more substantial to the child than she was herself – and she wanted in a sudden passion to break something. On impulse, using all her strength, she pushed at the recliner from behind, tipping it over slowly until it was upside down with its top resting on the carpet and its legs in the air, the rubber ferrules on the leg-ends unexpectedly silly in the moonlight, like prim, tiny shoes. Then she tipped over the painted chair too, so that its cushions flopped out, then pulled the wicker cone out of its frame and turned the frame over, flipped up the goatskin rug. She managed all this making hardly any noise, just a few soft bumps and thuds – yet when she had finished the room looked as if a storm had blown through it, throwing the chairs about.

She was shocked by what she'd effected, but gratified too; the after-sensation of strenuous work tingled in her legs and arms and in her chest, and she breathed fast; something wild in her whole body rejoiced in the chaos. Perhaps it would be funny when her parents saw it in the morning. At any rate nothing – *nothing* – would ever make her tell them that she'd done it. They would never know, and that was funny too. A private hilarity erupted in her, big bubbles struggling up out of her stomach which she mustn't give way to; she mustn't make any sound. And at that moment, while she surveyed her crazy handiwork, the moon sank below the top of the wall outside and the room darkened, all its solidity was withdrawn.

Her mother woke up early, in the dawn. Had her little boy called out to her? He sometimes woke in the night and had strange fits of crying when he didn't recognise her but screamed in her arms for his mummy. She listened, but heard nothing: yet she was as fully, promptly awake as if there'd been some summons, or a bell had rung. She felt as if something had happened while she was asleep. Carefully she sat up, not wanting to wake her sleeping husband lying with his knees drawn up and his back to her, the bristle of his crew cut – jet black hair against her white pillowcase – the only part of him visible above the blankets. The room was just as she had left it when she went to bed, except that his clothes were thrown on top of hers on the chair; he had stayed up late, working on his essay. She remembered dimly that when he got into the bed she had turned over, snuggling up to him, and that in her dream she had seemed to fit against the shape of his turned back and knees as sweetly as a nut into its shell, losing herself inside him: but now he was lost, where she couldn't follow him. Sometimes in the mornings, especially if they hadn't made love the night before, she would wake to this chilly sensation of finding herself beside a sleeping stranger, buried away from her fathoms deep, frowning in his sleep. His immobility then seemed like a comment, or a punishment, frightening her.

Everything in the bedroom was clearly visible and yet the grey light was still dilute and hesitant.

Even on sunny days these rooms at the front of the flat weren't bright. She had been very happy in this flat at first, in the new freedom of her married life; but now she resented the neighbours always brooding overhead, and was impatient to move out to a place they could have all to themselves. She had plans for just how she would transform the right house if they could find it, into something different and stylish; but the plans must wait until he'd finished his degree. She eased out from under the warmth of the blankets. Now she was thoroughly awake she needed to pee before she tried to sleep again: she would have to make the trek across the hall and out along the passageway which led from the front door, past the place where they kept their coats and boots and bikes, to the cold lavatory at the back of the house. When the children used the lavatory they liked her to wait by the hall door where they could still see her and she could call to them; sometimes she was frightened too, venturing down there at night, though she never told anyone.

Her reflection stood up indefatigably to meet her, as she got out of bed, in the gilt-framed mirror that was one of her junk shop finds, mounted in an alcove beside the window, with a trailing philodendron trained around it. It was too early to be on duty, seeing herself: she averted her eyes. Glimpsed at the corner of vision, though, the phantom in the baby-doll nightdress was enough like Monica Vitti (everyone said she looked like

Monica Vitti) to make her at least straighten up her back in self-respect – and she was aware, in the sleepy heat of her skin, of yesterday's *L'Air du Temps*. In the hall she listened at the door of the children's room, which stood just open – nothing. There was nothing to be afraid of. The lavatory was only banal and chilly: its tiny high window made it like a prison cell, but a blackbird sang liquidly outside in the back yard. On the way back to bed she looked into the kitchen, where everything was as she'd left it – he hadn't even made his cocoa, or eaten the sandwich she'd left, before he came to bed. His refraining made her tense her jaw, as if he repudiated her and preferred his work. She should have been a painter, she thought in a flash of anger, and not a housewife and a dressmaker – but at art college she'd been overawed by the Fine Artists who were grown men, experienced because they'd seen National Service in India and Malaya. The sight of her ordered kitchen in the dawn light reassured her: scene of her daily activity, poised and quiescent now, awaiting the morning when she'd pick it up again with renewed energy. Perhaps he might like bacon for his breakfast – she had saved up her housekeeping to buy him some. His mother had cooked him bacon every morning.

When she glanced into the lounge, her shock at the sight of the chairs thrown about in there was extreme as a hand clapped over her mouth from behind. The scene's mad violence was worse because it was frozen in silence – had lain in wait, gloating, while she suspected nothing. She was too afraid in the first moments to call out to her husband: the chaos seemed in itself an intruder close at hand, present like a snarling insult in her home. Someone had broken in. She waited in the doorway, holding her breath, for the movement that must give the intruder away: it was awful to know that a few minutes ago she had gone unprotected all the way down the lonely passageway to the lavatory. Then as her first panic subsided, she took in the odd specificity of the chaos: only the chairs were overturned at the centre of the room, nothing else was touched, nothing was pulled out from the shelves and thrown on the floor, nothing had been smashed. The lounge windows were tightly closed – just as the back door had surely been closed in the kitchen. Nothing had been taken. Had it? The wireless was intact on its shelf. Rousing out of her stupor she crossed to the desk and opened the drawer where her husband kept his band earnings. The money was safe: three pound ten in notes and some loose change, along with his pipe and pipe cleaners and dirty tobacco pouch, whose smell stayed on her fingers when she closed the drawer. The pages of his notes were untouched on the desk, too, where he'd left off from *Leviathan* the night before.

Instead of waking her husband, she tried the window catches, then went around checking the other rooms of the flat. The kitchen door and the front door were both securely bolted, and no one could have climbed in through the tiny window in the lavatory. Soundless on her bare feet, she entered the children's bedroom and stood listening to their breathing. Her little boy stirred in his sleep but didn't cry; her daughter was spread-eagled awkwardly amidst the menagerie of her stuffed toys and dolls. Their window, too, was fastened shut. There was no one inside the flat except themselves, and only one explanation for the crazy scene in the front room: her imagination danced with affront and dismay. Chilled, she returned to stand staring in the lounge. He was brooding and moody sometimes, and she'd always known he had this anger buried in him. But he'd never done anything like this before – nothing so naked and outrageous. She supposed he must have got frustrated with his studies, before he came to bed. Now everything was out in the open between them. Was the disorder a derisory message meant for her, because he despised her home-making, her domestication of the free life he once had? Or perhaps he was indifferent to what she thought of his anger. Perhaps the mess was even supposed to be some brutal kind of joke. She couldn't imagine how she had slept through its explosion: he must have dashed the chairs about as if a hurricane blew through the room.

This time, for once, she was definitely in the right, wasn't she? He was childish, giving way to his frustration – as if she didn't feel frustrated sometimes. And he criticised her for her bad temper! He had such high standards for everyone else's behaviour – but from now on she would always hold on to this new insight into him, no matter how reasonable he seemed. Her disdain hurt her, as if it bruised her chest – she was more used to admiring him. But it was also exhilarating: she seemed to see the future with great clarity, like looking forward into a long tunnel of antagonism, in which her husband was her enemy. And this awful truth appeared to be something she had always known – only in the past it had been shrouded in uncertainty, now she saw it starkly. Calmly and quietly she picked up each chair, put back the cushions which had tumbled onto the carpet, straightened the goatskin rug. The room looked as serene as if nothing had ever happened in it. The joke of its serenity erupted in her like bubbles of soundless laughter. Nothing – *nothing* – would ever make her acknowledge what he'd done, or the message he'd left for her; although when he saw the room restored to its rightful order, he must know that she knew. She would wait for him to acknowledge in words first, the passage of this silent violence between them.

Returning into the bedroom she lay down beside her husband with her back turned; her consciousness of her situation seemed very pure and brilliant and she expected to lie wide awake, burning from his nearness. There was less than an hour left of the night, before she had to get up to get all the others ready for school; she only got back into bed because her feet were cold and it was too early to switch on the electric fire in the kitchen. But almost at once she dropped into a deep sleep: particularly blissful, as if she were falling down and down through syrupy darkness, her limbs unbound and free and bathing in delicious warmth. When she woke again – this time her little boy really was calling out to her – she remembered immediately what had happened in the night, but she also felt refreshed and blessed.

A young wife fried bacon for her husband: the smell of it filled the flat. Her son was eating breakfast cereal at the table. Her husband was preoccupied, packing exercise books into his worn briefcase ready for school, opening the drawer in his desk in the lounge where he kept his pipe and tobacco, dropping these into the pocket of his tweed jacket with the leather patches on the elbows. But he came at some point to stand behind his wife at the stove where she was frying and put his arms around her, nuzzling her neck, kissing her behind her ear; and she leaned back into his kiss as she always did, tilting her head to give herself to him. When the bacon was ready she served it up on a plate with fried bread and a tomato and poured his tea, then went to find out why their daughter was dawdling in the bedroom. The little girl was sitting on the side of her brother's bunk, trying to pull on her knee-length socks with one hand while she held her book open with the other. Her thin freckled face was nothing like her mother's. One white sock was twisted all round her leg with its dirty heel sticking out at the front, and the book was surely the same one she had already read several times before. She was insistent, though, that she needed to start reading it at the beginning all over again. Her mother took the book away and chivvied her along.

The Taxidermist's Daughter

Francesca Rhydderch

THE WAY ALYCE told Ted about it later made it sound as if she'd meant to be rude, and he gave her a talking-to accordingly, but Daisy had been there too, slicing up giblets for her mother to make gravy. Who wanted a gentleman coming upon them like that, as Alyce said to Ted, looking at Daisy so she could nod her agreement, when you've got one hand holding a plucked goose to the kitchen table and the other trying to make sure its insides are scraped clean?

Ted listened, chewing, looking at what was left of the bird among its trimmings – Jerusalem artichokes, glazed parsnips, and the celeriac mash that no one had shown much of a taste for. It hadn't been a big goose: there were only the three of them now, after all, although there would be four again after New Year's Day, because the gentleman was taking lodgings with them.

–You wouldn't want that room at the top, Alyce had said to the professor when he'd made his enquiry, grimacing while she felt around between the goose's skin and breast, separating one from the other so she could push in spoonfuls of mashed cranberry and apple. –It's full of my husband's dead creatures. I'd have to clear them out.

–Oh no, please don't, he said. –I must insist you don't. It's my field, you see. I'm a naturalist by trade – Alyce frowned at that word, coming from this soft-whiskered gentleman – and it might be of use to me to observe your husband's specimens.

Alyce didn't stop massaging the goose with her red knuckles, and Daisy could tell she was thinking he might change his mind once he realised the room was filled to the rafters with creatures waiting to be sold. There was that case of birds from South America for one, sent home by a sea captain, with bee-eaters, hoopoes, kookaburras and even an S-necked flamingo crammed in beak to beak. His ship had gone down off Cape Horn, and they had ended up in the attic room, along with a fire screen made out of a peacock skin, and an albatross that had flown into the mast of a sailing ship.

Alyce had told the gentleman that theirs was not a comfortable house, what with all the comings and goings, people wanting to do business, mainly selling rather than buying, more's the pity, but he had kept on standing there, and when she paused for breath he asked if he could speak with Mr Reid and Alyce had been so – and, watching the look that passed between her parents as Alyce shared out the figgy pudding, Daisy thought to herself that her mother must still be feeling a little of the upset and temper she'd let slip under the gaze of the gentleman, for she blushed before carrying on – she'd been so *vexed* that she'd told him that if he was to lodge with them the first thing he must learn was to use the front door to the shop and not her kitchen door at the back. And he had tipped his hat and Daisy had taken him the long way round, out the back yard and down the lane to Bridge Street, keeping her head down.

Outside the shop it was just as her mother had said, people queuing up wanting to sell dead animals to her father. One man had a polecat as long as a python between his fingers, another a bittern that he held by the beak. He looked pleased with himself, despite the stench coming off the bird that surely meant it was far off being fresh. Most of them, though, had come straight from the beach where the petrels had been carried up on the tide after the storm, their tube noses frozen tight shut and their rigid white feathers flaked with patches of black, like snow in reverse. The men knew they wouldn't get more than a few shillings for them, but Ted was known for taking any small bird for a price. He always had a use for them, even if it was just in the background of a large case.

–You've got to set the scene, he'd say to Daisy, as she tried to hold her hand steady, painting a blue sky intended for the back of a display. –You can't just give people a stuffed creature and expect them to be done with it. They need action. Something about to happen.

–How can something be about to happen? Daisy said, concentrating on a cloudburst of yellow. –They're dead, aren't they?

–That doesn't matter. People need drama, dead or not, to make them want to look at the case again and again. What's the point of paying four pound for a swan in a box if you're barely going to look at it?

And so in Ted's boxes rabbits lolloped away from foxes who crouched over ledges, waiting to ambush or already pouncing on partridges with their preserved guts ripped open for all eternity. Butterflies, beetles and moths were everywhere, their fragile wings wide, terribly beautiful.

At the head of the queue outside the shop was Ted's stuffed bear standing up on its hind legs. It was his favourite creature, he said, because it was both exotic and attractive. Often small children would linger to stroke his fur as they went by, smiling at the silver tray set between his paws to make him look like a dumbwaiter. Daisy always thought of him as a him. His Lordship, David used to call him, wheeling him out onto the pavement each morning. The professor, though, projected no such airs and graces onto his Lordship; in fact, he barely gave him a second look, as if he were nothing more than a freakish creation set there to attract the attention of those who didn't know better.

Her father was standing in the middle of his workshop in his cloth cap and long white starched apron, with half-skinned animals lying all about him. There was a vixen on the table, pawing at his overall, her head to one side and her tongue hanging out – tongues were her father's specialty, each displaying a deep, grooved line cut down the middle with his smallest knife. She would be dry by now. All Ted had to do was push a pair of glass eyes into her preserved sockets – and Ted was particular, there were no teddy bear eyes for him; he would rather just plain black – then she would be ready for the case that Daisy had painted the day before. Sometimes when she slept she saw her father's stuffed creatures in her mind's eye, but in her dreams they moved, they panted, they whispered in her ear, strange things that made no sense to her, about there being no Heaven and Earth, nor life ever after, their forked tongues stroking her earlobe, making her body prickle all over, waking her up. She didn't tell her father about her dreams, nor even her mother. Alyce, she knew, would have said that *she* had no time to dream; *she* was tethered to the here and now.

–Father, Daisy said. There's a gentleman to see you. About the lodgings. She still didn't think of it as lodgings, the room at the top of the house. She thought of it as David's room.

She saw the professor looking up at an albino stoat hanging from a wire, its colourless ermine slowly hardening as it dried. –Incredible, he said. He put his hand into his pocket and brought out a red-and-white chequered handkerchief. He blew his nose, and kept the kerchief to it.

–You mustn't mind the smell, Sir, said Ted.

Daisy remembered that she hadn't liked it either, when she'd started working alongside her father, after David had left. She had been disgusted by the bits of decomposing flesh on the floor, which had to be swept up at the end of each day, and the commercial carpenter's glue her father favoured, with its stink of boiled hooves and bones. Ted had said she'd get used to it, and he was right. She watched the gentleman with some amusement.

–How long do they last?

–Forever, Sir, Ted said. –Daisy here tapes up the boxes, you see. Once they are taped up, those boxes, Sir, nothing can get at them. No air, no insects, nothing. They will live in those boxes forever. They'll never change. You could knock on this door in a hundred years and they'd still be here, just as they were the day we put them in their boxes, isn't it, Daisy?

–Yes, Father.

The gentleman looked at her, and at the paintbrush in her hand.

–Why do you make the sky so blue, young miss? It doesn't really look like that, does it?

Daisy wasn't sure if he was joking. He didn't smile, but he was staring at her as if he wouldn't leave off until she said something, so she gave him an answer as straight as she could.

–I'll paint it what colour I like, Sir. It's my sky, isn't it?

It was the professor's way, to ask questions. Not the kind of ignorant questions that customers asked: *Do you treat fur coats; how do you train passenger pigeons; can you teach me to fish?* The professor stood quietly, observing Ted at his worktop as he exchanged his calipers for his brain spoon, or replaced his poultry shears on the table and reached for his skinning hook. He would take note as Ted dipped his creatures in pickling saline and pasted them in borax. He would stand back as Ted removed individual hairs or feathers before gluing them on again, lips pursed like a dissatisfied hairdresser. Then he would start.

–You take care over your work, don't you?

–I have to, said Ted.

–Strange, though, that you have to go to such lengths to animate them. After all, you almost have to destroy each one completely before you put it back together.

It was true. By the time Ted had taken all the flesh out and replaced it with raw kapok and hemp padding, and pushed wires through it to hold it together, and stuck the skin back on, there was hardly any of it left, not as it had been, at least. And yet his creature, whatever it happened to be, looked perfect. Then he would bathe it in water with just a touch of arsenical soap to preserve it, tie threads all around it to squeeze the skin and feathers or fur into place, and hang it up to dry from the ceiling of the workshop.

–Where did you learn your trade, Sir? asked the professor.

–I was apprenticed to a big company in Birmingham. We saw all sorts there. Lions, tigers, you name it. My son – I sent him to be apprenticed there too – he even did an elephant once. It had lost an ear, though. Took him six weeks to make an artificial one.

The thought of David alive and well and not shot to smithereens, with his shirt sleeves rolled up and his face serious as he concentrated on pasting a pretend ear to a dead elephant, made something in the air between the three of them wrinkle up and fall to the floor in dried-out pieces, and Daisy turned back to her work, arranging sprigs of bulrushes in a long, thin case ready for the heron that had been found washed up on the mudflats down by the estuary. For if she was quick to finish her blue skies, she was also permitted to dip dried ferns in green paint and make rocks and crags out of papier-mâché. That was all, though. She couldn't ever touch the creatures.

–You need to pass your trade on, Sir, the professor said.

–I have passed it on. I passed it on to my son.

Ted never said David's name, but Daisy knew that the professor had heard it from Alyce. She'd seen her mother walking with him under the war memorial up at the castle.

The professor turned to Daisy, then, and started to tell her about the natural history museums he had visited, in London and New York, where they didn't dip ferns in paint or make stones out of papier-mâché, but went exploring, searching for the real thing, and bringing it back with them. They created exhibits that imitated nature exactly. You walked into those rooms and you could be in the jungle, he said.

–But who buys them, Sir?

–Oh, no one. People just come to look. To observe and to learn, he said.

–What is it they want to learn about, Sir?

–Ah, well now, there's a question. Nature in all her splendour, I'd say. The many mysteries that can now be divined due to modern science like your father's.

–But stuffing dead creatures isn't a science Sir, it's an art.

–Whoever told you that?

–My father.

–Very good, very good!

Both men laughed, and Daisy could see that Ted was making sure his own laugh was an exact reproduction of the professor's, drawn-out and mournful, like a donkey's. She laughed too, and Alyce, happening to come into the shop to give the professor his packed lunch, said how good it was to hear them all getting along together, and wouldn't it be nice if the professor came with them the next time they took a picnic up to Devil's Bridge on a Sunday afternoon? Ted, who had stopped laughing when she came in, said yes, indeed he must, and he, Ted, would of course lend the professor one of his guns, with pleasure.

They went up the Rheidol together on Easter Sunday, on the train. Alyce and Daisy stayed with the picnic basket while Ted and the professor went nesting. When Daisy caught sight of them coming back through the spinney, Alyce shook out an old blanket before laying it over the grass, which was still damp after the morning's rain. It felt strange sitting down on it so close together, passing round cracker boxes and tin cups. Daisy didn't know what to do with her legs; surely they hadn't been this long last time they'd come up here. Alyce stayed kneeling, she noticed, with her skirts tucked in at the sides so she could serve out the food with little trouble.

–Daisy loved coming here when she was small, Alyce said to the professor.

–Did I?

Daisy stared at her mother's face, trying to recall those times. A strand of hair was coming loose under Alyce's hat. Daisy couldn't remember what her mother was talking about, or if she did, the memories she had were flecked over with the grit that always got into her banana sandwiches, or the lemonade that spilled on her skirt, leaving a dark stain that smelled sour like urine when it dried, making her ashamed on the train on the way home.

–Don't you remember? You used to love playing hide-and-seek.

That had been with David. He was nothing more than an overgrown child, Alyce always used to say, smiling, watching him take off his socks and shoes and go splashing in the Mynach holding Daisy by the hand. When they came to dry off on the bank they would sit in the sun and look up at the three hoops of the bridge in silence, until David took one of his socks and made a hand puppet out of it, with wet pebbles for eyes, imitating difficult customers and making them all laugh, even Ted.

–Yes, I remember now, said Daisy.

And the sound was the same, the torrent of the waterfall, rushing down, down, into the cold, still pool at the bottom.

–David loved going rooking, didn't he, Mam? she said without thinking.

It was too late. His name was out there on the air like a bullet. Alyce sat in the centre of the blanket, her hat pulled off, her hair down her shoulders. Daisy tried to carry on chewing, but something was catching in her throat.

–The war showed him a life he'd thought he couldn't have, Alyce said to the professor, spooning out more of the pie onto his paper plate. –Away from here, stuffing Ted's dead creatures.

Ted didn't respond; he had seen something darting through the trees above and was lifting his gun to his shoulder.

–Ted shot an eagle on Tregaron bog the week after we got the telegram, Alyce went on. –Sold it for a mint to that museum down in Cardiff. It paid for David's funeral casket, that did.

The professor turned and looked at Daisy as

if it was her turn to say something – to remind the others perhaps of the beauty of the eagle with his dead feathers glistening, glued down at the sides. She opened her mouth to speak, but instead she found herself choking on her pie. She tried to draw breath. She could sense the damp earth pulsing underfoot, while inside her there was nothing. *No breath.* Up above, the sky slowly hardened into a suffocating dome. She choked again, feeling the stringy piece of meat caught in her windpipe now, moving neither up nor down, and small round pieces of lead shot on her tongue. *No breath.* They had all stopped moving: Ted, Alyce, and the professor. It was like looking at the world through glass.

The professor was standing right over her now. He dragged her up onto her feet and wrapped an arm around her stomach. With his other arm he pushed her forward, and struck her on the back several times with his fist. *No breath. No breath. No...*

And then everything was moving backwards, the piece of rook meat coming up into her mouth and flying through the air onto the grass, covered in spittle and vomit. The professor's fingers, clean and soapy, feeling their way along the groove of her tongue, picking away at the pieces of lead shot, plucking them out. And she was breathing, big gulps of warm blue air, fast at first, her heart still pumping far too hard, the blaring thrum of blood in her veins. Finally the sky started to ripple away from her, and the pleats of the hills gathered in, and

Alyce and Ted moved towards her.

–Don't say anything, Ted said to the professor over her head.

–About what? The professor sounded out of breath.

–About where the eagle came from.

–Sandwich, Sir? Alyce said.

And as Alyce held out a packet made out of stiff, waxed paper to the professor, Daisy got a waft of the celery salt that her mother always sprinkled over their chicken, and she felt hungry again, and put her hand out for one too.

When Daisy went into the studio the following morning everything was ready for her, laid out on Ted's worktop: scalpels, toe probes, splints, tail splitters and a sharpening stone. In the middle was a dead creature covered with a muslin cloth.

–What's this? she said.

The professor was smiling.

–Sit up there, Ted said. He gestured to his own high stool. He stood to one side, the professor to the other.

–Ready?

–Yes, she said, although she wasn't. The smell of saline pickle and tanning solution was too strong, even for her, and she was afraid she wouldn't be able to control her response, that she would be reduced to a creature herself, rearing and bucking and retching. She breathed out through her nose and held her lips clamped shut.

Ted pulled the muslin cloth away, and shook it out.

–Oh.

–What's wrong? Don't you know what it is? Come on, you've stood on the pier gawping at them enough times.

Daisy stared at the feathered body dotted with purples and greens.

–It can't be, she said. She was used to seeing starlings in their hundreds above the pier, their black silhouettes speckling the sky, collecting and separating like grains of sand in a timer.

–I thought they were your favourite, Ted said.

–They are.

–So let's see what you've learned from watching me.

He couldn't help showing off in front of the professor, Daisy thought, taking a piece of cotton and putting it in the bird's mouth.

She lifted the poor, dead creature up with one hand.

–Good, Ted said.

She folded the wings back gingerly, trying not to break any bones. A kaleidoscope of mauve and turquoise feathers slid over each other as they fanned open and shut. Ted took out a clean sheet of paper. Daisy turned the bird on its back and put it down on the sheet. She took the scalpel and made the opening cut along the almost bare flesh that ran from the breastbone the full length of its body. Slowly she worked her way all round it, freeing the skin, hearing it tear in places. She was sure she felt its soft bones tremble in her shaking hands.

–Keep going, said Ted, and then to the professor –You see that pink flesh there? That will need to come out.

The professor nodded, stepping closer and looking over her shoulder.

–What sex is it? he asked.

–Sex? Daisy thought. Sex was a word that she whispered to herself sometimes, in bed at night, to see how it sounded, or said in her head in chapel, watching it ricochet off the women's hats and the men's waistcoats, threatening to explode if it happened to get caught by the wrong person, by the minister, for example, who was delivering a sermon on the light that God shone over the darkness of the world. Sex was an indecent word, Alyce had told her.

Daisy felt it before she saw what she'd done, a soft giving from inside the starling where her blade had slipped and punctured its intestines. A runny mixture like porridge started to run out onto her fingers.

–Father!

–Control yourself, for God's sake, Ted shouted. –It's just bile, that's all it is.

He took the bird's skinned, leaking insides and made another cut down in the belly. He prodded and poked around inside for a minute with the tip of his scalpel. He peered over his glasses.

–Female, he said to the professor. –Look, you can see the ovaries, there.

Daisy knew that she had ovaries too, and a womb that bled every month into cloths which her mother boiled clean. It gave her an ache in her kidneys which her mother called growing pains. Sometimes she had to lie down in the afternoon and her mother brought her hot tea with lemon and told her to stay still until it had passed. She would feel hot and uncomfortable, being in bed at the wrong time of day, but Alyce would mop her face with cold water until she felt better.

–I'm sorry I made a mess of it, Father, she said.

–No matter. It's the outside that matters to us. I want you to write a label for me, then we'll wire up the legs.

Daisy sat up on the stool again and wrote the label out: ♀, *female.* She started to feel more cheerful. She was doing Ted's job, recreating nature with a fidelity that would bring her close to God. She was going to be greater than God perhaps, imbuing her creature with eternal life. She tried not to think of the joyous shapes the starlings made against the sky at sunset, and the rushing beat of their wings as they crowded down through the town's narrow streets, homing in on the sea.

The bell of the shop door rang out, and a draught of cool air cut through the gamey smell in the workshop. Ted went through to the front.

–Well done Daisy, said the professor, putting

one hand on her arm, making her smudge the paper a little. Her father liked his labels pristine, like everything else, but Daisy didn't care. When she went up to her room after lunch to brush her hair and wash her hands, she touched her arm where she had felt the professor's skin on hers. She couldn't see it but she could still feel it, the imprint of his fingers on the blue-threaded flesh at her wrist, marking her out as his.

Now that Daisy had put a name to the muddled arrangement of sensations that the professor provoked in her, they threatened to overwhelm her. She felt so full of them that she wondered sometimes if she had become the repository for all the life that had been sucked out of her father's dried-out creatures, if it had escaped like a newly released soul as Ted cut them from breastbone to navel, and come to land in her. When Alyce told her to give the professor another slice of toast, or to top up his coffee, Daisy hated her for making her go so close to him, close enough to see the weal on his cheek where he had nicked himself shaving, or the blue of his eyes like the sea on a clear day, navy and sharp. It was all right for Alyce, she thought, pushing the butter dish towards the professor; she had nothing to fill her mind apart from David, decently preserved memories that could be trusted to contain themselves. If Alyce looked over the kitchen table at the professor at all, it was only because that was where David used to sit. Whereas for Daisy, she could think only of the crook in the professor's elbow under his clean shirt sleeves, the way his voice seemed to vibrate through her when she was standing next to him, and the pain his silences caused her because she suspected they were filled with an ache that was for her alone.

Daisy's single starling was still in the shop window, waiting for a buyer. She wasn't to worry, Ted said, it would go before Whitsun, what with all the summer visitors coming to the seaside again. The trick, he said, was to forget all about one creature once it was over and done with, and to move on to the next one.

–Now, go and ask your mother for the sharpest knife she's got, he said. –Tell her I'll get her another one tomorrow.

–She'll be mad at you, Father. She won't be able to spare it.

–Just do as I say, child.

Daisy kicked the door frame as she went. No one had called her a child since the day of the wake. (Stupidest wake there ever was, if you asked him, Ted had said, what with there being no body and all, but the strangled sound his voice had made when he said it had betrayed him.) When Alyce had thrown herself across the coffin and cried – great racking, ugly howls – Ted had been embarrassed by the stares of the women gaggling with their cups of tea behind her. –Come along woman, he said; he's not even in there, is he? And it was true, because David had been shot to muddy pieces at the Somme, as the telegram had said, but his kit bag was in there that they'd found, and his spare uniform, with the clay brushed out of it by Alyce.

The kitchen door was shut. As she put her fingers to the handle, Daisy wondered about the silences between the four of them at the breakfast table each morning. The only person who didn't bring his dreams and nightmares to the table and lay them out in front of everyone was the professor. She felt like a specimen under his glass sometimes, wriggling as he inspected her, a body to be dissected. She wanted to know what went through his mind when he looked at her, if he felt a rush of what she now thought of as *sex* when she came into the kitchen in the mornings, her face still cold from the water she'd splashed over her eyes to stop them looking sleepy.

She was about to push the door open when something made her lean down and look through the keyhole instead. And there was Alyce, lying back on the kitchen table, gasping, once and then again and again, with the professor leaning over her, his trousers round his ankles, and Alyce's skirts falling about each side of his white, bony bottom. It had fine, blonde hairs on it, the kind Ted would have plucked out with a pair of tweezers and pasted back on after pickling the skin. The professor made a noise like a sob, and Daisy wished she could see his face, to see if he really was crying. She was glad to think that maybe this made him sad. He didn't love Alyce, with her big nipples, and her rolling stomach, and her hands that spent all day squeezing dough. The professor loved *her*, Daisy. One day, while Ted had been out the front taking payment for a tiger's head, all roaring, glazed orange fur with bleached white stripes, the professor had turned to Daisy and told her that he didn't want her to change, ever. What was it he'd said? –Wouldn't it be wonderful if we could all stay exactly as we are now, Daisy dear?

The professor and Alyce had stopped moving, but they were still breathing quickly and loudly, with puffs of flour falling in clouds all around them. The dirty breakfast dishes were heaped up by the sink, untouched.

Daisy crept upstairs to David's room. The door was open. She sat on the bed, which still held the warm shape of the professor in its unmade sheets. She looked round at her father's dead creatures in the shadows, their glass pupils black and unblinking and yet always staring back at you, until her own eyes hurt, and she cried. She stayed there for hours, not moving, not even when Ted called around the house for her, his voice strained and knowing, saying there was a man downstairs in the shop who wanted to buy her starling for his little boy.

She waited until the Sunday before May Day, when Alyce left her at home with a list of things to do in the kitchen while she and Ted went to chapel. The professor went to church, a tall, lonely building right by the sea, with a graveyard full of unsteady stones.

She mixed up the flour, eggs, sugar and butter to make speckled bread, and threw in the raisins as her mother did, by the handful, not counting or weighing them. She went through to the studio, pushed her way past the dumbwaiter bear who stood hulking in the shadows, stood on a chair and took down a box and a jar from the top shelf, marked *arsenical soap* and *arsenical powder*. Wearing her father's work gloves, she put a bar of the soap on the counter, cut a few fine slices, and dropped them into his special pan. She added a spoonful of the powdered arsenic and an ounce of camphor, and went back through to the kitchen, where she poured in a quart of cold water and boiled the mixture until the soap had melted. When it was ready she dropped a spoonful of it at a time into the cake mixture, and added a small jarful of glacé cherries. She knew the professor liked them especially. She'd heard him saying so to Alyce, how he adored licking their sticky, red perfection off his fingers, and Alyce laughing and saying she'd be sure to get him some more.

Once it was in the oven and the utensils had all been scrubbed and put away, Daisy glanced at the clock and went upstairs. She was thinking of going to lie down, just for a few minutes, but when she reached the top of the stairs, she found herself going up the next flight, to David's room.

It looked tidier than usual, and she wondered if Alyce had been in and turned down the bed and folded up his clothes. The case of birds from South America was gone – sold, finally, the week before – and there was a mark on the wall where it had stood. The desk was clear too, apart from a fountain pen, a pot of ink, and an exercise book.

Daisy sat down and opened the book. She'd never seen the professor's handwriting before. It wasn't like her father's, clean and slow for the sake of his customers. It ran about the place, all slopes and knots, with no need to think of anyone else, and she found it hard to keep up. She skipped through the entries quickly, the way she used to read poetry from the blackboard at school, not understanding everything, the teacher's ruler beating time on the desk at the front:

January 2nd: Mild, spring-like. Hedge Sparrow sang.
February 21st: Fine and bright in early part of afternoon. Hazel catkins only just out. Golden saxifrage buds not open yet. Missels singing. Heard a Ring Plover on the harbour mud.

She leafed through the pages, picking out single words, looking for her own name.

11th April, Easter Sunday:
Bad morning with squalls every few minutes. Went over to the Rheidol. The day cleared to some extent as we got to the divide, and rain held off for a good part of the morning. Waded the stream which ran deeper and stronger than the river, and up to the

Buzzards' nest behind the rowan tree. It was being relined ready for eggs. Left the Rheidol and held on alongside the big wood. Sighted Buzzards frequently. It was now dull again, and inclined to rain. Went into the wood. Soon found old Kites' nest which I had seen before. Then T. went up to a stick nest on chance but it proved to be a carrion's. Saw Greater Spotted Woodpecker. I noted some fine plants of Prickly Shield Fern, sheets of Filmy Fern, and Liverwort. Held on to the part of the wood away from the farm, and came to what I knew to be this year's nest at the top of a straight oak of 33ft. It was very near the spot where the nest up the crooked limb used to be. There was no doubt that we had a likely nest. I could not quite see into it from above, so T. went up. As he climbed I watched the evolutions of the bird. They were truly splendid: quills spread, their tips inclined upwards for the rising curve. Sometimes she threw over on the wind, falling backwards like a tumbler pigeon. Amidst great excitement, T. reported 2 eggs, quite contrary to my expectation, for I had no idea that they would be so early. He brought down the better egg of the two, marked chiefly towards the small end, and we felt that the fortune of the expedition was made. At the top of the wood we found an old Kite's nest built with big bits of sticks and lined with lamb skin, only eight feet from the ground. Ring Ouzel and Wheatons sang hopefully, but the lookout was bad enough. Rain eased off at lunchtime. Fine picnic at the waterfalls, marred only by T.'s daughter, who had a choking fit.

Further down the dale, three Buzzards came overhead, mothlike in the dusk. Back in triumph by the rail, dark and wet.

Daisy closed the book with care and put it back on the desk. The room went quiet.

He has no love in him, she thought.

Alyce's voice rose from the bottom of the house to the top, furious. That blessed fruit loaf was burned to a cinder, and where on earth was Daisy? An acrid smell spread through the house.

The professor left the morning after the bank holiday. Daisy woke with a plummeting feeling in her stomach that reminded her of David, a bewilderment that time could move forwards, carrying them all with it. She ran up and down the stairs, carrying ironed handkerchiefs and packed sandwiches up to the room at the top of the house.

–Daisy.

The professor came straight at her, closing the door behind her with one hand and putting the other onto her left breast. She thought he was going to kiss her, but he didn't. He ran his hand over her blouse as if he was trying to divine the living organism that was concealed underneath. She wanted to move but found she couldn't. Even when he took his hand away she didn't move.

–You didn't love that starling enough, you know, he said casually.

He laid the handkerchiefs on top of the shirts in his suitcase, turning away from her, dismissing her.

Everything in the room came to life then: the Swanson's hawk behind him, a scissor-tailed flycatcher, purple grackle, a deer's head on a neck mount, even a poorly stuffed brook trout (for Ted hated preserving fish; fish were for eating, he said), all breathing balefully at this man with no heart, their cornered black glass eyes burning into his soul. The professor felt it too, Daisy could swear he did. He looked over his shoulder as if he thought they were coming for him. He seemed frightened, his pasty face paler than the skin on his backside that day she'd seen him with her mother. She shook her head.

–I loved it too much, she said. –That was the trouble.

She stood at the shop door with Alyce, watching as Ted lifted the suitcase into the car and the professor got in on the passenger's side. She tried to call it to mind, the smell of the ruined fruit loaf, the heat and chaos of the kitchen, and everyone shouting at each other – Alyce having a go at her at her, and Ted telling her to pipe down, and Daisy saying that it wasn't her fault, none of it had been her fault, and the room itself on fire, it had felt like. She still remembered the sweat on her skin, and a tingling under her clothes, rage and *sex* close to the surface, and the professor's face grey like cold metal.

That night he had told them he was leaving: his fieldwork was done. Daisy remembered thinking what was she to do without him, with all these unruly emotions running through her and no single body to attach them to? Her mother had fed the burned cake to the birds, and dead seagulls had rained down onto the slate pavements.

The car was crossing the bridge now. Daisy tightened her grip on Alyce's arm.

Maybe, she thought, she would meet someone else. Maybe there would be another war and her parents would be glad she couldn't go away like David did. Maybe she would stay in the shop, stuff her father's dead creatures, make them all her own.

Caught by the sun as it climbed the road out of town, the car sent out one steely flare after another, picking up speed as it moved through the trees, passing through leaves that were frail in their blanched green freshness, improbably alive.

Kilifi Creek

Lionel Shriver

IT WAS A brand of imposition of which young people like Liana thought nothing: showing up on an older couple's doorstep, the home of friends of friends of friends, playing on a tentative enough connection that she'd have had difficulty constructing the sequence of referrals. If there was anything to that six-degrees-of-separation folderol, she must have been equally related to the entire population of the continent.

Typically, she'd given short notice, first announcing her intention to visit in a voicemail only a few days before bumming a ride with another party she hardly knew. (Well, the group had spent a long, hard-drinking night in Nairobi at a sprawling house with mangy dead animals on the walls that the guy with the ponytail was caretaking. In this footloose crowd of journalists and foreign-aid workers between famines, trust-fund layabouts, and tourists who didn't think of themselves as tourists if only because they never did anything, the evening qualified them all as fast friends.)

Ponytail Guy was driving to Malindi, on the Kenyan coast, for an expat bash that sounded a little druggie for Liana's Midwestern tastes. But the last available seat in his Land Rover would take her a stone's throw from this purportedly more-the-merrier couple and their gorgeously situated crash pad. It was nice of the guy to divert to Kilifi to drop her off, but then Liana was attractive, and knew it.

Mature adulthood—and the experience of being imposed upon herself—might have encouraged her to consider what showing up as an uninvited, impecunious house guest would require of her hosts. Though Liana imagined herself undemanding, even the easy to please required fresh sheets, which would have to be laundered after her departure, then dried and folded. She would require a towel for swimming, a second for her shower. She would expect dinner, replete with discreet refreshments of her wine glass, strong filtered coffee every morning, and—what cost older people more than a sponger in her early twenties realised—steady conversational energy channelled in her direction for the duration of her stay.

For her part, Liana always repaid such hospitality with brightness and enthusiasm. On arrival at the Henleys' airy, weathered wooden house nestled in the coastal woods, she made a point of admiring soapstone knick-knacks, cooing over framed black-and-whites of Masai initiation ceremonies, and telling comical tales about the European riffraff she'd met in Nairobi. Her effervescence came naturally. She would never have characterised it as an effort, until—and unless—she grew older herself.

While she'd have been reluctant to form the vain conceit outright, it was perhaps tempting to regard the sheer insertion of her physical presence as a gift, one akin to showing up at the door with roses. Supposedly a world-famous photographer, Regent Henley carried herself as if she used to be a looker, but she'd let her long dry hair go grey. Her crusty husband, Beano (the handle may have worked when he was a boy, but now that he was over sixty it sounded absurd), could probably use a little eye candy twitching onto their screened-in porch for sundowners: some narrow hips wrapped tightly in a fresh kikoi, long wet hair slicked back from a tanned, exertion-flushed face after a shower. Had Liana needed further rationalization of her amiable freeloading, she might also have reasoned that in Kenya every white household was overrun with underemployed servants. Not Regent and Beano but their African help would knot the mosquito netting over the guest bed. So Liana's impromptu visit would provide the domestics with something to do, helping to justify the fact that bwana paid their children's school fees.

But Liana thought none of these things. She thought only that this was another opportunity for adventure on the cheap, and at that time economy trumped all other considerations. Not because she was rude, or prone to take advantage by nature. She was merely young. A perfectly pleasant girl on her first big excursion abroad, she would doubtless grow into a better-socialised woman who would make exorbitant hotel reservations rather than dream of dumping herself on total strangers.

Yet midway through this casual mooching off the teeny-tiny-bit-pretentious photographer and her retired safari-guide husband (who likewise seemed rather self-impressed, considering that Liana had already run into a dozen masters of the savannah just like him), Liana entered one eerily elongated window during which her eventual capacity to make sterner judgments of her youthful impositions from the perspective of a more worldly adulthood became imperilled. A window after which there might be no woman. There might only, ever, have been a girl—remembered, guiltily, uneasily, resentfully, by her aging, unwilling hosts more often than they would have preferred.

Day Four. She was staying only six nights—an eye-blink for a twenty-three-year-old, a 'bloody long time' for the Brit who had groused to his wife under-breath about putting up 'another dewy-eyed Yank who confuses a flight to Africa with a trip to the zoo.' Innocent of Beano's less-than-charmed characterizations, Liana had already established a routine. Mornings were consumed with texting friends back in Milwaukee about her exotic situation, with regular refills of passion-fruit juice. After lunch, she'd pile into the jeep with Regent to head to town for supplies, after tolerating the photographer's ritual admonishment that Kilifi was heavily Muslim and it would be prudent to 'cover up.' (Afternoons were hot. Even her muscle T clung uncomfortably, and Liana considered it a concession not to strip down to her running bra. She wasn't about to drag on long pants to pander to a bunch of uptight foreigners she'd never see again; career expats like Regent were forever showing off how they're hip to local customs and you're not.) She never proffered a few hundred shillings to contribute to the grocery bill, not because she was cheap—though she was; at her age, that went without saying—but because the gesture never occurred to her. Back 'home,' she would mobilize for a long, vigorous swim in Kilifi Creek, where she would work up an appetite for dinner.

As she sidled around the house in her bikini—gulping more passion-fruit juice at the counter, grabbing a fresh towel—her exhibitionism was unconscious; call it instinctive, suggesting an inborn feel for barter. She lingered with Beano, inquiring about the biggest animal he'd ever shot, then commiserating about ivory poaching (always a crowd-pleaser) as she bound back her long blond hair, now bleached almost white. Raised arms made her stomach look flatter. Turning with a 'cheerio!' that she'd picked up in Nairobi, Liana sashayed out the back porch and down the splintered wooden steps before cursing herself, because she should have worn flip-flops. Returning for shoes would ruin her exit, so she picked her way carefully down the over-grown dirt track to the beach in bare feet.

In Wisconsin, a 'creek' was a shallow, burbling dribble with tadpoles that purled over rocks. Where Liana was from, you wouldn't go for a serious swim in a 'creek.' You'd splash up to your ankles while cupping your arches over mossy stones, arms extended for balance, though you almost always fell in. But everything in Africa was bigger. Emptying into the Indian Ocean, Kilifi Creek was a river—an impressively wide river at that—which opened into a giant lake sort of thing when she swam to the left and under the bridge. This time, in the interest of variety, she would strike out to the right.

The water was cold. Yipping at every advance, Liana struggled out to the depth of her upper thighs, gingerly avoiding sharp rocks. Regent and Beano may have referred to the shoreline as a 'beach,' but there wasn't a grain of sand in sight, and with all the green gunk along the bank obstacles were hard to spot. Chiding herself not to be a wimp, she plunged forward. This was a familiar ritual of her childhood trips to Lake Winnebago: the shriek of inhalation, the hyperventilation, the panicked splashing to get the blood running, the soft surprise of how quickly the water feels warm.

Liana considered herself a strong swimmer, of a kind. That is, she'd never been comfortable with the gasping and thrashing of the crawl, which felt frenetic. But she was a virtuoso of the sidestroke, with a powerful scissor kick whose thrust carried her faster than many swimmers with inefficient crawls (much to their annoyance, as she'd verified in her college pool). The sidestroke was contemplative. Its rhythm was ideally calibrated for a breath on every other kick, and resting only one cheek in the water allowed her to look around. It was less rigorous than the butterfly but not as geriatric as the breaststroke, and after long enough you still got tired—marvellously so.

Pulling out far enough from the riverbank so that she shouldn't have to worry about hitting rocks with that scissor kick, Liana rounded to the right and rapidly hit her stride. The late-afternoon light had just begun to mellow. The shores were forested, with richly shaded inlets and copses. She didn't know the names of the trees, but now that she was alone, with no one trying to make her feel ignorant about a continent of which white people tended to be curiously possessive, she didn't care if those were acacias or junipers. They were green: good enough. Though Kilifi was renowned as a resort area for high-end tourists, and secreted any number of capacious houses like her hosts', the canopy hid them well. It looked like wilderness: good enough. Gloriously, Liana didn't have to watch out for the powerboats and Jet Skis that terrorised Lake Winnebago, and she was the only swimmer in sight. Africans, she'd been told (lord, how much she'd been *told*; every backpacker three days out of Jomo Kenyatta airport was an expert), didn't swim. Not only was the affluent safari set too lazy to get in the water; by this late in the afternoon they were already drunk.

This was the best part of the day. No more enthusiastic chatter about Regent's latest work. For heaven's sake, you'd think she might have finally discovered colour photography at this late date. Blazing with yellow flora, red earth, and, at least outside Nairobi, unsullied azure sky, Africa was wasted on the woman. All she photographed was dust and poor people. It was a relief, too, not to have to seem fascinated as Beano lamented the unsustainable growth of the human population and the demise of Kenyan game, all the while having to pretend that she hadn't heard variations on this same dirge dozens of times in a mere three weeks. Though she did hope that, before she hopped a ride back to Nairobi with Ponytail Guy, the couple would opt for a repeat of that antelope steak from the first night. The meat had been lean; rare in both senses of the word, it gave good text the next morning. There wasn't much point in going all the way to Africa and then sitting around eating another hamburger.

Liana paused her reverie to check her position, and sure enough she'd drifted farther from the shore than was probably wise. She knew from the lake swims of childhood vacations that distance over water was hard to judge. If anything, the shore was farther away than it looked. So she pulled heavily to the right, and was struck by how long it took to make the trees appear appreciably larger. Just when she'd determined that land was within safe reach, she gave one more stiff kick, and her right foot struck rock.

The pain was sharp. Liana hated interrupting a swim, and she didn't have much time before the equatorial sun set, as if someone had flicked a light switch. Nevertheless, she dropped her feet and discovered that this section of the creek was barely a foot and a half deep. No wonder she'd hit a rock. Sloshing to a sun-warmed outcrop, she examined the top of her foot, which began to gush blood as soon as she lifted it out of the water. There was a flap. Something of a mess.

Even if she headed straight back to the Henleys', all she could see was thicket—no path, much less a road. The only way to return and put some kind of dressing on this stupid thing was to swim. As she stumbled through the shallows, her foot smarted. Yet, bathed in the cool water, it quickly grew numb. Once she had slogged in deep enough to resume her sidestroke, Liana reasoned, *Big deal, I cut my foot*. The water would keep the laceration clean; the chill would stanch the bleeding. It didn't really hurt much now, and the only decision was whether to cut the swim short. The silence pierced by tropical birdcalls was a relief, and

Liana didn't feel like showing up back at the house with too much time to kill with enraptured blah-blah before dinner. She'd promised herself that she'd swim at least a mile, and she couldn't have done more than a quarter.

So Liana continued to the right, making damned sure to swim out far enough so that she was in no danger of hitting another rock. Still, the cut had left her rattled. Her idyll had been violated. No longer gentle and welcoming, the shoreline shadows undulated with a hint of menace. The creek had bitten her. Having grown fitful, the sidestroke had transformed from luxury to chore. Possibly she'd tightened up from a queer encroaching fearfulness, or perhaps she was suffering from a trace of shock—unless, that is, the water had genuinely got colder. Once in a while she felt a flitter against her foot, like a fish, but it wasn't a fish. It was the flap. Kind of creepy.

Liana resigned herself: this expedition was no longer fun. The light had taken a turn from golden to vermillion—a modulation she'd have found transfixing if only she were on dry land—and she still had to swim all the way back. Churning a short length farther to satisfy pride, she turned around.

And got nowhere. Stroking at full power, Liana could swear she was going backward. As long as she'd been swimming roughly in the same direction, the current hadn't been noticeable. This was a *creek*, right? But an African creek. As for her having failed to detect the violent surge running at a forty-five-degree angle to the shoreline, an aphorism must have applied—something about never being aware of forces that are on your side until you defy them.

Liana made another assessment of her position. Her best guess was that the shore had drifted farther away again. Very much farther. The current had been pulling her out while she'd been dithering about the fish-flutter flap of her foot. Which was now the least of her problems. Because the shore was not only distant. It stopped.

Beyond the end of the land was nothing but water. Indian Ocean water. If she did not get out of the grip of the current, it would sweep her past that last little nub of the continent and out to sea. Suddenly the dearth of boats, Jet Skis, fellow-swimmers, and visible residents or tourists, drunken or not, seemed far less glorious.

The sensation that descended was calm, determined, and quiet, though it was underwritten by a suppressed hysteria that it was not in her interest to indulge. Had she concentration to spare, she might have worked out that this whole emotional package was one of her first true tastes of adulthood: what happens when you realize that a great deal or even everything is at stake and that no one is going to help you. It was a feeling that some children probably did experience but shouldn't. At least solitude discouraged theatrics. She had no audience to panic for. No one to exclaim to, no one to whom she might bemoan her quandary. It was all do, no say.

Swimming directly against the current had proved fruitless. Instead, Liana angled sharply toward the shore, so that she was cutting across the current. Though she was still pointed backward, in the direction of Regent and Beano's place, this riptide would keep dragging her body to the left. Had she known her exact speed, and the exact rate at which the current was carrying her in the direction of the Indian Ocean, she would have been able to answer the question of whether she was about to die by solving a simple geometry problem: a point travels at a set speed at a set angle toward a plane of a set width while moving at a set speed to the left. Either it will intersect the plane or it will miss the plane and keep travelling into wide-open space. Liquid space, in this case.

Of course, she wasn't in possession of these variables. So she swam as hard and as steadily as she knew how. There was little likelihood that suddenly adopting the crawl, at which she'd never been any good, would improve her chances, so the sidestroke it would remain. She trained her eyes on a distinctive rock formation as a navigational guide. Thinking about her foot wouldn't help, so she did not. Thinking about how exhausted she was wouldn't help, so she did not. Thinking about never having been all that proficient at geometry was hardly an assist, either, so she proceeded in a state of dumb animal optimism.

The last of the sun glinted through the trees and winked out. Technically, the residual threads of pink and grey in the early-evening sky were very pretty.

'Where is that blooming girl?' Beano said, and threw one of the leopard-print cushions onto the sofa. 'She should have been back two hours ago. It's dark. It's Africa, she's a baby, she knows absolutely nothing, and it's dark.'

'Maybe she met someone, went for a drink,' Regent said.

'Our fetching little interloper's *meeting someone* is exactly what I'm afraid of. And how's she to go to town with some local rapist in only a bikini?'

'You would remember the bikini,' Regent said dryly.

'Damned if I understand why all these people rock up and suddenly they're our problem.'

'I don't like it any more than you do, but if she floats off into the night air never to be seen again she is our problem. Maybe someone picked her up in a boat. Carried her round the southern bend to one of the resorts.'

'She'll not have her phone on a swim, so she's no means of giving us a shout if she's in trouble. She'll not have her wallet, either—if she even has one. Never so much as volunteers a bottle of wine, while hoovering up my best Cabernet like there's no tomorrow.'

'If anything has happened, you'll regret having said that sort of thing.'

'Might as well gripe while I still can, then. You know, I don't even know the girl's surname? Much less who to ring if she's vanished. I can see it: having to comb through her kit, search out her passport. Bringing in the sodding police, who'll expect chai just for answering the phone. No good ever comes from involving those thieving idiots in your life, and then there'll be a manhunt. Thrashing the bush, prodding the shallows. And you know how the locals thrive on a mystery, especially when it involves a young lady—'

'They're bored. We're all bored. Which is why you're letting your imagination run away with you. It's not that late yet. I'm sure there's a simple explanation.'

'I'm not bored, I'm hungry. Aziza probably started dinner at four—since she *is* bored—and you can bet it's muck by now.'

Regent fetched a bowl of fried-chick-pea snacks, but despite Beano's claims of an appetite he left them untouched. 'Christ, I can see the whole thing,' he said, pacing. 'It'll turn into one of those cases. With the parents flying out and grilling all the servants and having meetings with the police. Expecting to stay here, of course, tearing hair and getting emotional while we urge them to please do eat some lunch. Going on tirades about how the local law enforcement is ineffectual and corrupt, and bringing in the F.B.I. Telling childhood anecdotes about their darling and expecting us to get tearful with them over the disappearance of some, I concede, quite agreeable twenty-something, but still a girl we'd barely met.'

'You like her,' Regent said. 'You're just ranting because you're anxious.'

'She has a certain intrepid quality, which may be deadly, but which until it's frightened out of her I rather admire,' he begrudged, then resumed the rant. 'Oh, and there'll be media. CNN and that. You know the Americans—they love innocent-abroad stories. But you'd think they'd learn their lesson. It beats me why their families keep letting kids holiday in Africa as if the whole world is a happy-clappy theme park. With all those car-jackings on the coast road—'

'Ordinarily I'd agree with you, but there's nothing especially *African* about going for a swim in a creek. She's done it every other afternoon, so I've assumed she's a passable swimmer. Do you think—would it help if we got a torch and went down to the dock? We could flash it about, shout her name out. She might just be lost.'

'My throat hurts just thinking about it.' Still, Beano was heading to the entryway for his jacket when the back-porch screen door creaked.

'Hi,' Liana said shyly. With luck, streaks of mud and a strong tan disguised what her weak, light-headed sensation suggested was a shocking pallor. She steadied herself by holding onto the sofa and got mud on the upholstery. 'Sorry,

I—swam a little farther than I'd planned. I hope you didn't worry.'

'We *did* worry,' Regent said sternly. Her face flickered between anger and relief, an expression that reminded Liana of her mother. 'It's after dark.'

'I guess with the stars, the moon...' Liana covered. 'It was so... peaceful.'

The moon, in fact, had been obscured by cloud for the bulk of her wet grope back. Most of which had been conducted on her hands and knees in shallow water along the shore—land she was not about to let out of her clutches for one minute. The muck had been treacherous with more biting rocks. For long periods, the vista had been so inky that she'd found the Henleys' rickety rowboat dock only because she had bumped into it.

'What happened to your *foot*?' Regent cried.

'Oh, that. Oh, nuts. I'm getting blood on your floor.'

'Looks like a proper war wound, that,' Beano said boisterously.

'We're going to get that cleaned right up.' Examining the wound, Regent exclaimed, 'My dear girl, you're shaking!'

'Yes, I may have gotten—a little chill.' Perhaps it was never too late to master the famously British knack for understatement.

'Let's get you into a nice hot shower first, and then we'll bandage your foot. That cut looks deep, Liana. You really shouldn't be so casual about it.'

Liana weaved to the other side of the house, leaving red footprints down the hall. In previous showers here, she'd had trouble with scalding, but this time she couldn't get the water hot enough. She huddled under the dribble until finally the water grew tepid, and then, with a shudder, wrapped herself in one of their big white bath sheets, trying to keep from getting blood on the towel.

Emerging in jeans and an unseasonably warm sweater she'd found in the guest room's dresser, Liana was grateful for the cut on her foot, which gave Regent something to fuss over and distracted her hostess from the fact that she was still trembling. Regent trickled the oozing inch-long gash with antiseptic and bound it with gauze and adhesive tape, whose excessive swaddling didn't make up for its being several years old; the tape was discoloured, and barely stuck. Meanwhile, Liana threw the couple a bone: she told them how she had injured her foot, embellishing just enough to make it a serviceable story.

The foot story was a decoy. It obviated telling the other one. At twenty-three, Liana hadn't accumulated many stories; until now, she had hungered for more. Vastly superior to carvings of hippos, stories were the very souvenirs that this bold stint in Africa had been designed to provide. Whenever she'd scored a proper experience in the past, like the time she'd dated a man who confided that he'd always felt like a woman, or even when she'd had her e-mail hacked, she'd traded on the tale at every opportunity. Perhaps if she'd returned to her parents after this latest ordeal, she'd have burst into tears and delivered the blow-by-blow. But she was abruptly aware that these people were virtual strangers. She'd only make them even more nervous about whether she was irresponsible or lead them to believe that she was an attention-seeker with a tendency to exaggerate. It was funny how when some little nothing went down you played it for all it was worth, but when a truly momentous occurrence shifted the tectonic plates in your mind you kept your mouth shut. Because instinct dictated that this one was private. Now she knew: there was such a thing as private.

Having aged far more than a few hours this evening, Liana was disheartened to discover that maturity could involve getting smaller. She had been reduced. She was a weaker, more fragile girl than the one who'd piled into Regent's jeep that afternoon, and in some manner that she couldn't put her finger on she also felt less real—less here—since in a highly plausible alternative universe she was not here.

The couple made a to-do over the importance of getting hot food inside her, but before the dinner had warmed Liana curled around the leopard-print pillow on the sofa and dropped into a comatose slumber. Intuiting something—Beano himself had survived any number of close calls, the worst of which he had kept from Regent, lest she lay down the law that he had to stop hunting in Botswana even sooner than she did—he discouraged his wife from rousing the girl even to go to bed, draping her gently in a mohair blanket and carefully tucking the fringe around her pretty wet head.

Predictably, Liana grew into a civilized woman with a regard for the impositions of laundry. She pursued a practical career in marketing in New York, and, after three years, ended an impetuous marriage to an Afghan. Meantime, starting with Kilifi Creek, she assembled an offbeat collection. It was a class of moments that most adults stockpile: the times they almost died. Rarely was there a good reason, or any warning. No majestic life lessons presented themselves in compensation for having been given a fright. Most of these incidents were in no way heroic, like the rescue of a child from a fire. They were more a matter of stepping distractedly off a curb, only to feel the draught of the M4 bus flattening your hair.

Not living close to a public pool, Liana took up running in her late twenties. One evening, along her usual route, a minivan shot out of a parking garage without checking for pedestrians and missed her by a whisker. Had she not stopped to double-knot her left running shoe before leaving her apartment, she would be dead. Later: She was taking a scuba-diving course on Cape Cod when a surge about a hundred feet deep dislodged her mask and knocked her regulator from her mouth. The Atlantic was unnervingly murky, and her panic was absolute. Sure, they taught you to make regular decompression stops, and to exhale evenly as you ascended, but it was early in her training. If her instructor hadn't managed to grab her before she bolted for the surface while holding her breath, her lungs would have exploded and she would be dead. Still later: Had she not unaccountably thought better of lunging forward on her Citi Bike on Seventh Avenue when the light turned green, the garbage truck would still have taken a sharp left onto Sixteenth Street without signalling, and she would be dead. There was nothing else to learn, though that was something to learn, something inchoate and large.

The scar on her right foot, wormy and white (the flap should have been stitched), became a totem of this not-really-a-lesson. Oh, she'd considered the episode, and felt free to conclude that she had overestimated her swimming ability, or underestimated the insidious, bigger-than-you powers of water. She could also sensibly have decided that swimming alone anywhere was tempting fate. She might have concocted a loftier version, wherein she had been rescued by an almighty presence who had grand plans for her—grander than marketing. But that wasn't it. Any of those interpretations would have been plastered on top, like the poorly adhering bandage on that gash.

The message was bigger and dumber and blunter than that, and she was a bright woman, with no desire to disguise it.

After Liana was promoted to director of marketing at BraceYourself—a rapidly expanding firm that made the neoprene joint supports popular with aging boomers still pounding the pavement—she moved from Brooklyn to Manhattan, where she could now afford a stylish one-bedroom on the twenty-sixth floor, facing Broadway. The awful Afghan behind her, she'd started dating again. The age of thirty-seven marked a good time in her life: she was well paid and roundly liked in the office; she relished New York; though she'd regained an interest in men, she didn't feel desperate. Many an evening without plans she would pour a glass of wine, take the elevator to the top floor, and slip up a last flight of stairs; roof access was one of the reasons she'd chosen the apartment. Especially in summertime, the regal overlook made her feel rich beyond measure. Lounging against the railing sipping Chenin Blanc, Liana would bask in the lights and echoing taxi horns of the city, sometimes sneaking a cigarette. The air would be fat and soft in her hair—which was shorter now, with a becoming cut. So when she finally met a man whom she actually liked, she invited him to her building's traditional Fourth of July potluck picnic on the roof to show it off.

'Are you sure you're safe, sitting there?' David said solicitously. They had sifted away from the tables of wheat-berry salad and smoked-tofu patties to talk.

His concern was touching; perhaps he liked her, too. But she was perfectly stable—lodged against the perpendicular railing on a northern corner, feet braced on a bolted-down bench, weight firmly forward—and her consort had nothing to fear. Liana may have grown warier of water, but heights had never induced the vertigo from which others suffered. Besides, David was awfully tall, and the small boost in altitude was equalising.

'You're just worried that I'll have a better view of the fireworks. Refill?' She leaned down for the Merlot on the bench for a generous pour into their plastic glasses. A standard fallback for a first date, they had been exchanging travel stories, and impetuously—there was something about this guy that she trusted—she told him about Kilifi Creek. Having never shared the tale, she was startled by how little time it took to tell. But that was the nature of these stories: they were about what could have happened, or should have happened, but didn't. They were very nearly not stories at all.

'That must have been pretty scary,' he said dutifully. He sounded let down, as if she'd told a joke without a punch line.

'I wasn't scared,' she reflected. 'I couldn't afford to be. Only later, and then there was no longer anything to be afraid of. That's part of what was interesting: having been cheated of feeling afraid. Usually, when you have a near-miss, it's an instant. A little flash, like, *Wow. That was weird*. This one went on forever, or seemed to. I was going to die, floating off on the Indian Ocean until I lost consciousness, or I wasn't. It was a long time to be in this... in-between state.' She laughed. 'I don't know, don't make me embarrassed. I've no idea what I'm trying to say.'

Attempting to seem captivated by the waning sunset, Liana no more than shifted her hips, by way of expressing her discomfort that her story had landed flat. Nothing foolhardy. For the oddest moment, she thought that David had pushed her, and was therefore not a nice man at all but a lunatic. Because what happened next was both enormously subtle and plain enormous—the way the difference between knocking over a glass and not knocking over a glass could be a matter of upsetting its angle by a single greater or lesser degree. Greater, this time. Throw any body of mass that one extra increment off its axis, and rather than barely brush against it you might as well have hurled it at a wall.

With the same quiet clarity with which she had registered in Kilifi, *I am being swept out to sea*, she grasped simply, *Oh. I lost my balance.* For she was now executing the perfect back flip that she'd never been able to pull off on a high dive. The air rushed in her ears like water. This time the feeling was different—that is, the starkness was there, the calmness was there also, but these clean, serene sensations were spiked with a sharp surprise, which quickly morphed to perplexity, and then to sorrow. She fit in a wisp of disappointment before the fall was through. Her eyes tearing, the lights of high-rises blurred. Above, the evening sky rippled into the infinite ocean that had waited to greet her for fourteen years: largely good years, really—gravy, a long and lucky reprieve. Then, of course, what had mattered was her body striking the plane, and now what mattered was not striking it—and what were the chances of that? By the time she reached the sidewalk, Liana had taken back her surprise. At some point there was no *almost*. That had always been the message. There were bystanders, and they would get the message, too.

Miss Adele Amidst the Corsets

Zadie Smith

'WELL, THAT'S THAT,' Miss Dee Pendency said, and Miss Adele, looking back over her shoulder, saw that it was. The strip of hooks had separated entirely from the rest of the corset. Dee held up the two halves, her big red slash mouth pulling in opposite directions.

'Least you can say it died in battle. Doing its duty.'

'Bitch, I'm on in ten minutes.'

'*When an irresistible force like your ass...*'

'Don't sing.'

'*Meets an old immovable corset like this... You can bet as sure as you liiiiiive!*'

'It's your fault. You pulled too hard.'

'*Something's gotta give, something's gotta give, SOMETHING'S GOTTA GIVE.*'

'You pulled too hard.'

'Pulling's not your problem.' Dee lifted her bony, white Midwestern leg up onto the counter, in preparation to put on a thigh-high. With a heel she indicated Miss Adele's mountainous box of chicken and rice: 'Real talk, baby.'

Miss Adele sat down on a grubby velvet stool before a mirror edged with blown-out bulbs. She was thickening and sagging, in all the same ways, in all the same places, as her father. Plus it was midwinter: her skin was ashy. She felt like some once-valuable piece of mahogany furniture lightly dusted with cocaine. This final battle with her corset had set her wig askew. She was forty-six years old.

'Lend me yours.'

'Good idea. You can wear it on your arm.'

And tired to death, as the Italians say—tired to *death*. Especially sick of these kids, these 'millennials,' or whatever they were calling themselves. Always on. No backstage to any of them—only front of house. Wouldn't know a sincere, sisterly friendship if it kicked down the dressing-room door and sat on their faces.

Miss Adele stood up, untaped, put a furry deerstalker on her head, and switched to her comfortable shoes. She removed her cape. Maybe stop with the cape? Recently she had only to catch herself in the mirror at a bad angle, and there was Daddy, in his robes.

'The thing about undergarments,' Dee said, 'is they can only do so much with the cards they've been dealt. Sorta like Obama?'

'Stop talking.'

Miss Adele zipped herself into a cumbersome floor-length padded coat, tested—so the label claimed—by climate scientists in the Arctic.

'Looking swell, Miss Adele.'

'Am I trying to impress somebody? Tell Jake I went home.'

'He's out front—tell him yourself!'

'I'm heading this way.'

'You know what they say about choosing between your ass and your face?'

Miss Adele put her shoulder to the fire door and heaved it open. She caught the punch line in the ice-cold stairwell.

'You should definitely choose one of those at some point.'

Aside from the nights she worked, Miss Adele tried not to mess much with the East Side. She'd had the same sunny rent-controlled studio apartment on Tenth Avenue and Twenty-Third since '93, and loved the way the West Side communicated with the water and the light, loved the fancy galleries and the big anonymous condos, the High Line funded by bankers and celebrities, the sensation of clarity and wealth. She read the real estate section of the *Times* with a kind of religious humility: the news of a thirty-four-million-dollar townhouse implied the existence of a mighty being, out there somewhere, yet beyond her imagining. But down here? Depressing. Even worse in the daylight. Crappy old buildings higgledy-piggledy on top of each other, ugly students, shitty pizza joints, delis, tattoo parlours. Nothing bored Miss Adele more than ancient queens waxing lyrical about the good old bad old days. At least the bankers never tried to rape you at knifepoint or sold you bad acid. And then once you got past the Village, everything stopped making sense. Fuck these little streets with their dumbass names! Even the logistics of googling her location—remove gloves, put on glasses, find the phone—were too much to contemplate in a polar vortex. Instead, Miss Adele stalked violently up and down Rivington, cutting her eyes at any soul who dared look up. At the curb she stepped over a frigid pool of yellow fluid, three paper plates frozen within it. What a dump! Let the city pull down everything under East Sixth, rebuild, number it, make it logical, pack in the fancy hotels—not just one or two but a whole bunch of them. Don't half gentrify—follow through. Stop preserving all this old shit. Miss Adele had a right to her opinions. Thirty years in a city gives you the right. And now that she was, at long last, no longer beautiful, her opinions were all she had. They were all she had left to give to people. Whenever her disappointing twin brother, Devin, deigned to call her from his three-kids-and-a-Labradoodle, goofy-sweater-wearing, golf-playing, liberal-Negro-wet-dream-of-a-Palm-Springs-fantasy existence, Miss Adele made a point of gathering up all her hard-won opinions and giving them to him good. 'I wish he could've been mayor forever. FOR-EVAH. I wish he was my boyfriend. I wish he was my daddy.' Or: 'They should frack the hell out of this whole state. We'll get rich, secede from the rest of you dope-smoking, debt-ridden assholes. You the ones dragging us all down.' Her brother accused Miss Adele of turning rightward in old age. It would be more accurate to say that she was done with all forms of drama—politics included. That's what she liked about gentrification, in fact: gets rid of all the drama.

And who was left, anyway, to get dramatic about? The beloved was gone, and so were all the people she had used, over the years, as substitutes for the beloved. Every kid who'd ever called her gorgeous had already moved to Brooklyn, Jersey, Fire Island, Provincetown, San Francisco, or the grave. This simplified matters. Work, paycheck, apartment, the various lifestyle sections of the *Times*, Turner Classic Movies, Nancy Grace, bed. Boom. Maybe a little *Downton*. You needn't put your face on to watch *Downton*. That was her routine, and disruptions to it—like having to haul ass across town to buy a new corset—were rare. Sweet Jesus, this cold! Unable to feel her toes, she stopped a shivering young couple in the street. British tourists, as it turned out; clueless, nudging each other and beaming up at her Adam's apple with delight, like she was in their guidebook, right next to the Magnolia Bakery and the Naked Cowboy. They had a map, but without her glasses it was useless. They had no idea where they were. 'Sorry! Stay warm!' they cried, and hurried off, giggling into their North Face jackets. Miss Adele tried to remember that her new thing was that she positively liked all the tourists and missed Bloomberg and loved Midtown and the Central Park nags and all the Prada stores and *The Lion King* and lining up for cupcakes wherever they happened to be located. She gave those British kids her most winning smile. Sashayed round the corner in her fur-cuffed Chelsea boots with the discreet heel. Once out of sight, though, it all fell apart; the smile, the straightness of her spine, everything. Even if you don't mess with it—even when it's not seven below—it's a tough city. New York just expects so much from a girl—acts like it can't stand even the *idea* of a wasted talent or opportunity. And Miss Adele had been around. Rome says: enjoy me. London: survive me. New York: gimme all you got. What a thrilling proposition! The chance to be 'all that you might be.' Such a thrill—until it becomes a burden. To put a face on—to put a self on—this had once been, for Miss Adele, pure delight. And part of the pleasure had been precisely this: the buying of things. She used to love buying things! Lived for it! Now it felt like effort, now if she never bought another damn thing again she wouldn't even—

Clinton Corset Emporium. No awning, just a piece of cardboard stuck in the window. As Miss Adele entered, a bell tinkled overhead—an actual bell, on a catch wire—and she found herself in a long narrow room—a hallway really—with a counter down the left-hand side and a curtained-off cubicle at the far end, for privacy. Bras and corsets were everywhere, piled on top of each other in anonymous white cardboard boxes, towering up to the ceiling. They seemed to form the very walls of the place.

'Good afternoon,' said Miss Adele, daintily removing her gloves, finger by finger. 'I am looking for a corset.'

A radio was on; talk radio—incredibly loud. Some AM channel bringing the latest from a distant land, where the people talk from the back of their throats. One of those Eastern-y, Russian-y places. Miss Adele was no linguist, and no geographer. She unzipped her coat, made a noise in the back of her own throat, and looked pointedly at the presumed owner of the joint. He sat slumped behind the counter, listening to this radio with a tragic twist to his face, like one of those sad-sack cab drivers you see hunched over the wheel, permanently tuned in to the bad news from back home. And what the point of that was, Miss Adele would never understand. Turn that shit down! Keep your eyes on the road! Lord knows, the day Miss Adele stepped out of the state of Florida was pretty much the last day that godforsaken spot ever crossed her mind.

Could he even see her? He was angled away, his head resting in one hand. Looked to be about Miss Adele's age, but further gone: bloated face, about sixty pounds overweight, bearded, religious type, wholly absorbed by this radio of his. Meanwhile, somewhere back there, behind the curtain, Miss Adele could make out two women talking:

'Because she thinks Lycra is the answer to everything. Why you don't speak to the nice lady? She's trying to help you. She just turned fourteen.'

'So she's still growing. We gotta consider that. Wendy—can you grab me a Brava 32B?'

A slip of an Asian girl appeared from behind the curtain, proceeded straight to the counter and vanished below it. Miss Adele turned back to the owner. He had his fists stacked like one potato, two potato—upon which he rested his chin—and his head tilted in apparent appreciation of what Miss Adele would later describe as 'the ranting'—for did it not penetrate every corner of that space? Was it not difficult to ignore? She felt she had not so much entered a shop as some stranger's spittle-filled mouth. RAGE AND RIGHTEOUSNESS, cried this radio—in whatever words it used—RIGHTEOUSNESS AND RAGE. Miss Adele crossed her arms in front of her chest, like a shield. Not this voice—not today. Not any day—not for Miss Adele. And though she had learned, over two decades, that there was nowhere on earth entirely safe from the voices of rage and righteousness—not even the new New York—still Miss Adele had taken great care to organize her life in such a way that her encounters with them were as few as possible. (On Sundays, she did her groceries in a cutoff T-shirt that read thou shalt.) As a child, of course, she had been fully immersed—dunked in the local water—with her daddy's hand on the back of her head, with his blessing in her ear. But she'd leaped out of that shallow channel the first moment she was able.

'A corset,' she repeated, and raised her spectacular eyebrows. 'Could somebody help me?'

'WENDY,' yelled the voice behind the curtain, 'could you see to our customer?'

The shopgirl sprung up, like a jack-in-the-box, clutching a stepladder to her chest.

'Looking for Brava!' shouted the girl over the radio, turned her back on Miss Adele, opened the stepladder, and began to climb it. Meanwhile, the owner shouted something at the woman behind the curtain, and the woman, adopting his tongue, shouted something back.

'It is customary, in retail—' Miss Adele began.

'Sorry—one minute,' said the girl, came down with a box underarm, dashed right past Miss Adele, and disappeared once more behind the curtain.

Miss Adele took a deep breath. She stepped back from the counter, pulled her deerstalker off her head, and tucked a purple bang behind her ear. Sweat prickled her face for the first time in weeks. She was considering turning on her heel and making that little bell shake till it fell off its goddamn string when the curtain opened and a mousy girl emerged, with her mother's arm around her. They were neither of them great beauties. The girl had a pissy look on her face and moved with an angry slouch, like a prisoner, whereas you could see the mother was at least trying to keep things civilized. The mother looked beat—and too young to have a teenager. Or maybe she was the exact right age. Devin's kids were teenagers. Miss Adele was almost as old as the president. None of this made any sense, and yet you were still expected to accept it, and carry on, as if it were the most natural process in the world.

'Because they're not like hands and feet,' a warm and lively voice explained, from behind the curtain. 'They grow independently.'

'Thank you so much for your advice, Mrs. Alexander,' said the mother, the way you talk to a priest through a screen. 'The trouble is this thickness here. All the women in our family got it, unfortunately. Curved rib cage.'

'But actually, you know—it's inneresting—it's a totally different curve from you to her. Did you realize that?'

The curtain opened. The man looked up sharply. He was otherwise engaged, struggling with the antennae of his radio to banish the static, but he paused a moment to launch a little invective in the direction of a lanky, wasp-waisted woman in her early fifties, with a long, humane face—dimpled, self-amused—and an impressive mass of thick chestnut hair.

'Two birds, two stones,' said Mrs. Alexander, ignoring her husband, 'that's the way we do it here. Everybody needs something different. That's what the big stores won't do for you. Individual attention. Mrs. Berman, can I give you a tip?' The young mother looked up at the long-necked Mrs. Alexander, a duck admiring a swan. 'Keep it on all the time. Listen to me, I know of what I speak. I'm wearing mine right now, I wear it every day. In my day they gave it to you when you walked out of the hospital!'

'Well, you look amazing.'

'Smoke and mirrors. Now, all you need is to make sure the straps are fixed right like I showed you.' She turned to the sulky daughter and put a fingertip on each of the child's misaligned shoulders. 'You're a lady now, a beautiful young lady, you—' Here again she was interrupted from behind the counter, a sharp exchange of mysterious phrases, in which—to Miss Adele's satisfaction—the wife appeared to get the final word. Mrs. Alexander took a cleansing breath and continued: 'So you gotta hold yourself like a lady. Right?' She lifted the child's chin and placed her hand for a moment on her cheek. 'Right?' The child straightened up despite herself. See, some people are trying to ease your passage through this world—so ran Miss Adele's opinion—while others want to block you at every turn. Think of poor Mama, taking folk round those god-awful foreclosures, helping a family to see the good life that might yet be lived there—that had just as much chance of sprouting from a swamp in the middle of nowhere as anyplace else. That kind of instinctive, unthinking care. If only Miss Adele had been a simple little fixer-upper, her mother might have loved her unconditionally! Now that Miss Adele had grown into the clothes of middle-aged women, she noticed a new feeling of affinity toward them, far deeper than she had ever felt for young women, back when she could still fit into the hot pants of a showgirl. She walked through the city struck by middle-aged women and the men they had freely chosen, strange unions of the soft and the hard. In shops, in restaurants, in line at the CVS. She always had the same question. Why in God's name are you still married to this asshole? Lady, your children are grown. You have your own credit cards. You're the one with life force. Can't you see he's just wallpaper? It's not 1850. This is New York. Run, baby, run!

'Who's waiting? How can I help you?'

Mother and daughter duck followed the shopgirl to the counter to settle up. The radio, after a brief pause, made its way afresh up the scale of outrage. And Miss Adele? Miss Adele turned like a flower to the sun.

'Well, I need a new corset. A strong one.'

Mrs. Alexander beamed: 'Come right this way.'

Together, they stepped into the changing area. But as Miss Adele reached to pull the curtain closed behind them both—separating the ladies from the assholes—a look passed between wife and husband

and Mrs. Alexander caught the shabby red velvet swathe in her hand, a little higher up than Miss Adele had, and held it open.

'Wait—let me get Wendy in here.' An invisible lasso, thought Miss Adele. He throws it and you go wherever you're yanked. 'You'll be all right? The curtain's for modesty. You modest?'

Oh, she had a way about her. Her face expressed emotion in layers: elevated, ironic eyebrows, mournful violet eyes, and sly, elastic mouth. Miss Adele could have learned a lot from a face like that. A face straight out of an old movie. But which one, in particular?

'You're a funny lady.'

'A life like mine, you have to laugh—Marcus, please, one minute—' He was barking at her, still—practically insisting, perhaps, that she *stop talking to that schwarze*, which prompted Mrs. Alexander to lean out of the changing room to say something very like: *What is wrong with you? Can't you see I'm busy here?* On the radio, strange atonal music replaced the ranting; Mrs. Alexander stopped to listen to it, and frowned. She turned back to her new friend and confidante, Miss Adele. 'Is it okay if I don't measure you personally? Wendy can do it in a moment. I've just got to deal with—but listen, if you're in a hurry, don't panic, our eyes, they're like hands.'

'Can I just show you what I had?'

Miss Adele unzipped her handbag and pulled out the ruin.

'Oh! You're breaking my heart! From here?'

'I don't remember. Maybe ten years ago?'

'Makes sense, we don't sell these any more. Ten years is ten years. Time for a change. What's it to go under? Strapless? Short? Long?'

'Everything. I'm trying to hide some of this.'

'You and the rest of the world. Well, that's my job.' She leaned over and put her lips just a little shy of Miss Adele's ear: 'What you got up there? You can tell me. Flesh or feathers?'

'Not the former.'

'Got it. WENDY! I need a Futura and a Queen Bee, corsets, front fastening, forty-six. Bring a forty-eight, too. Marcus—please. One *minute*. And bring the Paramount in, too! The crossover! Some people,' she said, turning to Miss Adele, 'you ask them these questions, they get offended. Everything offends them. Personally, I don't believe in 'political correctness.'' She articulated the phrase carefully, with great sincerity, as if she had recently coined it. 'My mouth's too big. I gotta say what's on my mind! Now, when Wendy comes, take off everything to here and try each corset on at its tightest setting. If you want a defined middle, frankly it's going to hurt. But I'm guessing you know that already.'

'Loretta Young,' called Miss Adele to Mrs. Alexander's back. 'You look like Loretta Young. Know who that is?'

'Do I know who Loretta Young is? Excuse me one minute, will you?'

Mrs. Alexander lifted her arms comically, to announce something to her husband, the only parts of which Miss Adele could fully comprehend were the triple repetition of the phrase 'Loretta Young.' In response, the husband made a noise somewhere between a sigh and a grunt.

'Do me a favour,' said Mrs. Alexander, letting her arms drop and turning back to Miss Adele, 'put it in writing, put it in the mail. He's a reader.'

The curtain closed. But not entirely. An inch hung open and through it Miss Adele watched a silent movie—silent only in the sense that the gestures were everything. It was a marital drama, conducted in another language, but otherwise identical to all those she and Devin had watched as children, through a crack in the door of their parents' bedroom. God save Miss Adele from marriage! Appalled, fascinated, she watched the husband, making the eternal, noxious point in a tone Miss Adele could conjure in her sleep (*You bring shame upon this family*), and Mrs. Alexander, apparently objecting (*I've given my life to this family*); she watched as he became belligerent (*You should be ashamed*) and she grew sarcastic (*Ashamed of having a real job? You think I don't know what 'pastoral care' means? Is that God's love you're giving to every woman in this town?*), their voices weaving in and out of the hellish noise on the radio, which had returned to ranting (*THOU SHALT NOT!*).

Miss Adele strained to separate the sounds into words she might google later. If only there was an app that translated the arguments of strangers! A lot of people would buy that app. Hadn't she just been reading in the *Times* about some woman who had earned eight hundred grand off such an app—just for having the idea for the app. You want to know what Miss Adele would do with eight hundred grand? Buy a studio down in Battery Park, and do nothing all day but watch the helicopters fly over the water. Stand at the floor-to-ceiling window, bathed in expensive light, wearing the kind of silk kimono that hides a multitude of sins.

Sweating with effort and anxiety, in her windowless Lower East Side cubicle, Miss Adele got stuck again at her midsection, which had become, somehow, Devin's midsection. Her fingers fumbled with the heavy-duty eyes and hooks. She found she was breathing heavily. ABOMINATION, yelled the radio. *Get it out of my store!* cried the man, in all likelihood. *Have mercy!* pleaded the woman, basically. No matter how she pulled, she simply could not contain herself. So much effort! She was making odd noises, grunts almost.

'Hey, you okay in there?'

'First doesn't work. About to try the second.'

'No, don't do that. Wait. Wendy, get in there.'

In a second, the girl was in front of her, and as close as anybody had been to Miss Adele's bare body in a long time. Without a word, a little hand reached out for the corset, took hold of one side of it and, with surprising strength, pulled it toward the other end until both sides met. The girl nodded, and this was Miss Adele's cue to hook the thing together while the girl squatted like a weight lifter and took a series of short, fierce breaths. Outside of the curtain, the argument had resumed.

'Breathe,' said the girl.

'They always talk to each other like that?' asked Miss Adele.

The girl looked up, uncomprehending.

'Okay now?'

'Sure. Thanks.'

The girl left Miss Adele alone to examine her new silhouette. It was as good as it was going to get. She turned to the side and frowned at three days of chest stubble. She pulled her shirt over her head to see the clothed effect from the opposite angle, and in the transition got a fresh view of the husband, still berating Mrs. Alexander, though in a violent whisper. He had tried bellowing over the radio; now he would attempt to tunnel underneath it. Suddenly he looked up at Miss Adele—not as far as her eyes, but tracing, from the neck down, the contours of her body. RIGHTEOUSNESS, cried the radio, RIGHTEOUSNESS AND RAGE! Miss Adele felt like a nail being hammered into the floor. She grabbed the curtain and yanked it shut. She heard the husband end the conversation abruptly—as had been her own father's way—not with reason or persuasion, but with sheer volume. Above the door to the emporium the little bell rang.

'Molly! So good to see you! How're the kids? I'm just with a customer!' Mrs. Alexander's long pale fingers curled round the hem of the velvet. 'May I?'

Miss Adele opened the curtain.

'Oh, it's good! See, you got shape now.'

Miss Adele shrugged, dangerously close to tears: 'It works.'

'Marcus said it would. He can spot a corset size at forty paces, believe me. He's good for that at least. So, if that works, the other will work. Why not take both? Then you don't have to come back for another twenty years! It's a bargain.' She turned to shout over her shoulder, 'Molly, I'm right with you,' and threw open the curtain.

In the store there had appeared a gaggle of children, small and large, and two motherly looking women, who were greeting the husband and being greeted warmly in turn, smiled at, truly welcomed. Miss Adele picked up her enormous coat and began the process of re-weatherising herself. She observed Mrs. Alexander's husband as he reached over the counter to joke with two young children, ruffling their hair, teasing them, while his wife—whom she watched even more intently—stood smiling over the whole phony operation, as if all that had passed between him and her were nothing at all, some silly wrangle about the accounts or whatnot. Oh, Loretta Young. Whatever you need to tell yourself, honey. Family first! A phrase that sounded, to Miss Adele, so broad, so empty; one of those convenient pits into which folk will throw any and everything they can't deal with alone. A hole for cowards to hide in. Under its cover you could even have your hands round your wife's throat, you could have your terrified little boys cowering in a corner—yet when the bell rings, it's time for iced tea and 'Family First!' with all those nice churchgoing ladies as your audience, and Mama's cakes, and smiles all round. *These are my sons, Devin and Darren.* Two shows a day for seventeen years.

'I'll be with you in one minute, Sarah! It's been so long! And look at these girls! They're really tall now!'

On the radio, music again replaced the voice—strange, rigid, unpleasant music, which seemed to Miss Adele to be entirely constructed from straight lines and corners. Between its boundaries, the vicious game restarted, husband and wife firing quick volleys back and forth, at the end of which he took the radio's old-fashioned dial between his fingers and turned it up. Finally Mrs. Alexander turned from him completely, smiled tightly at Miss Adele, and began packing her corsets back into their boxes.

'Sorry, but am I causing you some kind of issue?' asked Miss Adele, in her most discreet tone of voice. 'I mean, between you and your...'

'You?' said Mrs. Alexander, and with so innocent a face Miss Adele was tempted to award her the Oscar right then and there, though it was only February. 'How do you mean, issue?'

Miss Adele smiled.

'You should be on the stage. You could be my warm-up act.'

'Oh, I doubt you need much warming. No, you don't pay me, you pay him.' A small child ran by Mrs. Alexander with a pink bra on his head. Without a word she lifted it, folded it in half, and tucked the straps neatly within the cups. 'Kids. But you gotta have life. Otherwise the whole thing moves in one direction. You got kids?'

Miss Adele was so surprised, so utterly wrong-footed by this question, she found herself speaking the truth.

'My twin—he has kids. We're identical. I guess I feel like his kids are mine, too.'

Mrs. Alexander put her hands on her tiny waist and shook her head.

'Now, that is *fascinating*. You know, I never thought of that before. Genetics is an amazing thing—amazing! If I wasn't in the corset business, I'm telling you, that would have been my line. Better luck next time, right?' She laughed sadly, and looked over at the counter. 'He listens to his lectures all day, he's educated. I missed out on all that.' She picked up the two corsets packed back into their boxes. 'Okay, so—are we happy?'

Are *you* happy? Are you really happy, Loretta Young? Would you tell me if you weren't, Loretta Young, the Bishop's Wife? Oh, Loretta Young, Loretta Young! Would you tell anybody?

'Molly, don't say another word—I know exactly what you need. Nice meeting you,' said

Mrs. Alexander to Miss Adele, over her shoulder, as she took her new customer behind the curtain. 'If you go over to my husband, he'll settle up. Have a good day.'

Miss Adele approached the counter and placed her corsets upon it. She stared down a teenage girl leaning on the counter to her left, who now, remembering her manners, looked away and closed her mouth. Miss Adele returned her attention to the side of Mrs. Alexander's husband's head. He picked up the first box. He looked at it as if he'd never seen a corset box before. Slowly he wrote something down in a note pad in front of him. He picked up the second and repeated the procedure, but with even less haste. Then, without looking up, he pushed both boxes to his left, until they reached the hands of the shopgirl, Wendy.

'Forty-six fifty,' said Wendy, though she didn't sound very sure. 'Um... Mr. Alexander—is there discount on Paramount?'

He was in his own world. Wendy let a finger brush the boss's sleeve, and it was hard to tell if it was this—or something else—that caused him to now sit tall in his stool and thump a fist upon the counter, just like Daddy casting out the devil over breakfast, and start right back up shouting at his wife—some form of stinging question—repeated over and over, in that relentless way men have. Miss Adele strained to understand it. Something like: *You happy now?* Or: *Is this what you want?* And underneath, the unmistakable: *Can't you see he's unclean?*

'Hey, you,' said Miss Adele, 'Yes, you, sir. If I'm so disgusting to you? If I'm so beneath your contempt? Why're you taking my money? Huh? You're going to take my money? *My* money? Then, please: look me in the eye. Do me that favour, okay? Look me in the eye.'

Very slowly a pair of profoundly blue eyes rose to meet Miss Adele's own green contacts. The blue was unexpected, like the inner markings of some otherwise unremarkable butterfly, and the black lashes were wet and long and trembling. His voice, too, was the opposite of his wife's, slow and deliberate, as if each word had been weighed against eternity before being chosen for use.

'You are speaking to me?'

'Yes, I'm speaking to you. I'm talking about customer service. Customer service. Ever hear of it? I am your customer. And I don't appreciate being treated like something you picked up on your shoe!'

The husband sighed and rubbed at his left eye.

'I don't understand—I say something to you? My wife, she says something to you?'

Miss Adele shifted her weight to her other hip and very briefly considered a retreat. It did sometimes happen, after all—she knew from experience—that is, when you spent a good amount of time alone—it did sometimes come to pass—when trying to decipher the signals of others—that sometimes you mistook—

'Listen, your wife is friendly—she's civilized, I ain't talking about your wife. I'm talking about *you*. Listening to your... whatever the hell that this—your *sermon*—blasting through this store. You may not think I'm godly, brother, and maybe I'm not, but I am in your store with good old-fashioned American money and I ask that you respect that and you respect me.'

He began on his other eye, same routine.

'I see,' he said, eventually.

'Excuse me?'

'You understand what is being said, on this radio?'

'*What*?'

'You speak this language that you hear on the radio?'

'I don't *need* to speak it to understand it. And why you got it turned up to eleven? I'm a customer—whatever's being said, I don't want to listen to that shit. I don't need a translation—I can hear the *tone*. And don't think I don't see the way you're looking at me. You want to tell your wife about that? When you were peeping at me through that curtain?'

'Now I'm looking at you?'

'Is there a problem?' said Mrs. Alexander. Her head came out from behind the curtain.

'I'm not an idiot, okay?' said Miss Adele.

The husband brought his hands together, somewhere between prayer and exasperation, and shook them at his wife as he spoke to her, over Miss Adele's head, and around her comprehension.

'Hey—talk in English. English! Don't disrespect me! Speak in English!'

'Let me translate for you: I am asking my wife what she did to upset you.'

Miss Adele turned and saw Mrs. Alexander, clinging to herself and swaying, less like Loretta now, more like Vivien Leigh swearing on the red earth of Tara.

'I'm not talking about her!'

'Sir, was I not polite and friendly to you? Sir?'

'First up, I ain't no sir—you live in this city, use the right words for the right shit, okay?'

There was Miss Adele's temper, bad as ever. She'd always had it. Even before she was Miss Adele, when she was still little Darren Bailey, it had been a problem. Had a tendency to go off whenever she felt herself on uncertain ground, like a cheap rocket—the kind you could buy back home in the same store you bought a doughnut and a gun. Short fused and likely to explode in odd, unpredictable directions, hurting innocent bystanders—often women, for some reason. How many women had stood opposite Miss Adele with the exact same look on their faces as Mrs. Alexander wore right now? Starting with her mother and stretching way out to kingdom come. The only Judgment Day that had ever made sense to Miss Adele was the one where all the hurt and disappointed ladies form a line—a chorus line of hurt feelings—and one by one give you your pedigree, over and over, for all eternity.

'Was I rude to you?' asked Mrs. Alexander, the colour rising in her face, 'No, I was not. I live, I let live.'

Miss Adele looked around at her audience. Everybody in the store had stopped what they were doing and fallen silent.

'I'm not talking to you. I'm trying to talk to this gentleman here. Could you turn off that radio so I can talk to you, please?'

'Okay,' he said, 'so maybe you leave now.'

'Second of all,' said Miss Adele, counting it out on her hand, though there was nothing to follow in the list, 'contrary to appearances, and just as a point of information, I am not an Islamic person? I mean, I get it. Pale, long nose. But no. So you can hate me, fine—but you should know who you're hating and hate me for the right reasons. Because right now? You're hating in the wrong direction—you and your radio are wasting your hate. If you want to hate me, file it under N-word. As in African American. Yeah.'

The husband frowned and held his beard in his hand.

'You are a very confused person. I don't care what you are. All such conversations are very boring to me, in fact.'

'Oh, I'm *boring* you?'

'Honestly, yes. And you are also being rude. So now I ask politely: leave, please.'

'Baby, I am out that door, believe me. But I am not leaving without my motherfucking corsets.'

The husband slipped off his stool, finally, and stood up.

'You leave now, please.'

'Now, who's gonna make me? 'Cause you can't touch me, right? That's one of your laws, right? I'm unclean, right? So who's gonna touch me? Miss Tiny Exploited Migrant Worker over here?'

'Hey, I'm international student! NYU!'

Et tu, Wendy? Miss Adele looked sadly at her would-be ally. Wendy was a whole foot taller now, thanks to the stepladder, and she was using the opportunity to point a finger in Miss Adele's face. Miss Adele was tired to death.

'Just give me my damn corsets.'

'Sir, I'm sorry but you really have to leave now,' said Mrs. Alexander, walking toward Miss Adele, her elegant arms wrapped around her itty-bitty waist. 'There are minors in here, and your language is not appropriate.'

'Y'all call me 'sir' one more time,' said Adele, speaking to Mrs. Alexander, but still looking at the husband, 'I'm gonna throw that radio right out that fucking window. And don't you be thinking I'm an anti-Semite or some shit...' Miss Adele faded. She had the out-of-body sense that she was watching herself on the big screen, at one of those screenings she used to attend, with the beloved boy, long dead, who'd adored shouting at the screen, back when young people still went to see old movies in a cinema. Oh, if that boy were alive! If he could see

Miss Adele up on that screen right now! Wouldn't he be shouting at her performance—wouldn't he groan and cover his eyes! The way he had at Joan and Bette and Barbara, as they made their terrible life choices, all of them unalterable, no matter how loudly you shouted.

'It's a question,' stated Miss Adele, 'of simple politeness. Po-lite-ness.'

The husband shook his shaggy head and laughed, softly.

'See, you're trying to act like I'm crazy, but from the moment I stepped up in here, you been trying to make me feel like you don't want someone like me up in here—why you even denying it? You can't even look at me now! I know you hate black people. I know you hate homosexual people. You think I don't know that? I can look at you and know that.'

'But you're wrong!' cried the wife.

'No, Eleanor,' said the husband, putting out a hand to stop the wife continuing, 'maybe she's a divinity. Maybe she sees into the hearts of men.'

'You know what? It's obvious this lady can't speak for herself when you're around. I don't even want to talk about this another second. My money's on the counter. This is twenty-first-century New York. This is America. And I've paid for my goods. Give me my goods.'

'Take your money and leave. I ask you politely. Before I call the police.'

'I'm sure he'll go peacefully,' predicted Mrs.

Alexander, tearing the nail of her index finger between her teeth, but, instead, one more thing went wrong in Miss Adele's mind, and she grabbed those corsets right out of poor Wendy's hands, kicked the door of Clinton Corset Emporium wide open, and hightailed it down the freezing street, slipped on some ice and went down pretty much face-first. After which, well, she had some regrets, sure, but there wasn't much else to do at that point but pick herself up and run, with a big, bleeding dramatic graze all along her left cheek, wig askew, surely looking to everyone she passed exactly like some Bellevue psychotic, a hot crazy mess, an old-school deviant from the fabled city of the past—except, every soul on these streets was a stranger to Miss Adele. They didn't have the context, didn't know a damn thing about where she was coming from, nor that she'd paid for her goods in full, in dirty green American dollars, and was only taking what was rightfully hers.

The American Lover

Rose Tremain

1.

ALL DAY LONG, lying on the sofa in the sitting room of her parents' London Mansion flat, Beth hears the clunk of the elevator doors opening and closing.

Sometimes, she hears voices on the landing – people arriving or departing – and then the long sigh of the elevator descending. She wishes there were no people, no elevator, no pain. She stares at the old-fashioned room. She stares at her crutches, propped up against a wing chair. In a few months' time she is going to be thirty.

There is a Portuguese maid, Rosalita, who comes in at two o'clock every day.

She is never late. Rosalita has a gentle face and plump, downy arms. As she sprays the furniture with beeswax polish, she will often talk about her old life, and this is the only thing that Beth enjoys – hearing about Rosalita's old life in a garment factory in Setubal, making costumes for matadors. The places Rosalita describes are hot and bright and filled with the sound of sewing machines or brass musical instruments. She describes how the matadors used to flirt with the seamstresses. They were young, she says, and full of ardour and their sweat was scented with incense, from the number of visits they made to the bull ring chapels. These things remind Beth that there were days long ago when she was innocent enough to worship the ordinary beauty of the world.

★

In 1964, the lover came.

He was American. His name was Thaddeus. He came in and looked at Beth, who was nineteen years old. He was forty-eight, the same age as Beth's father. He was a commercial photographer, but when he saw Beth, with her serious, exquisite face, he said: 'I have to photograph you.'

Beth knew that she shouldn't go near him, that his skin would burn her, that his kiss would silence her. But she went.

Her mother said to her: 'I know what you're doing. I haven't told your father. I really think you should end this. He's much too old for you. It's shameful.'

But all Beth could think was, I love this shame. I'm on fire with shame. My shame is an electric pulse so strong, it could bring the dead to life.

Thaddeus had an estranged wife named Tricia, an ex-model who lived in California.

Something he liked to do with Beth was to describe the many ways he used to make love to Tricia. Sometimes, at moments of wild intensity, he called Beth 'Tricia'. But Beth didn't mind. She could be anyone he chose: Beth, Tricia, Julie Christie, Jean Shrimpton, Jeanne Moreau, Brigitte Bardot… it didn't matter. Whatever self she'd had before she met him was invisible to her now. At certain moments in a life, this is what a person can feel. She was her lover's lover, that was all.

While Rosalita is dusting Beth's crutches, which she does very tenderly, from time to time, Beth shows her pictures from her press file.

The picture Rosalita likes best is of the car. It's in colour. There's nobody in the photograph, just the car, parked on the gravel of the house Beth once owned in the South of France: a pillar-box-red E-Type Jaguar soft-top with wire wheels. Rosalita shakes her head and whispers, 'Beautiful car.'

And Beth says one day, 'You know, Rosalita, there was a time when it was very easy for me to buy a car like that. In fact, it was given to me, but I could have bought it. I had all the money in the world.'

Thaddeus had no money. Only what the earned from his photography for the ad agencies of domestic appliances and food and hotel exteriors and yachts and London bobbies on bicycles, wearing what he called 'those droll Germanic helmets'.

'Jealousy of David Bailey,' joked Thaddeus, 'is my only flaw.'

Beth looked at him. He was thin and dark. There were dusty patches of grey in his chest hair. He let his toenails grow too long. He was beginning to go bald. There were times when Beth thought, He's just a very ordinary man. He doesn't have the grand, sinewy neck of Charlton Heston or the swooning brown eyes of Laurence Olivier. He's not even tall. But she knew that none of this made the least difference to her feelings.

In the car crash, Beth's legs had been broken in five places. They had been the legs of a dancer, strong and limber, shapely and thin. Now, her bones were bolted together with metal and coffined in plaster of Paris. What they would look like when the plaster of Paris was one day cut away, Beth couldn't imagine. She thought they might resemble the legs of a home-made rag doll, or those floppy limbs the women seem to have in paintings by Chagall, and that forever more, she would have to be carried through life in the arms of people who were whole.

Sometimes, while Rosalita is trying to clean the flat, the power goes off. This is now 1974 and the Three Day Week is going on. 'All caused,' says Beth's father, 'by the bloody NUM. Trade unions hold this country to ransom.'

Though Rosalita shakes her head in frustration when the Hoover falls suddenly silent, she has sympathy for the coal miners, towards whom Beth is indifferent, just as she is indifferent to everything else. Rosalita and Beth smoke Peter Stuyvesant cigarettes in front of the gas fire – Beth on the sofa, Rosalita on the floor – and try to imagine what the life of a coal miner might be like.

'The thing I wouldn't mind,' says Beth, 'is the darkness.'

'Darkness maybe OK,' says Rosalita, 'But there is also the heat and the dirt and the risk of the fire.'

'Fire?'

'Fire from methane gas. Fire coming out of the tunnel wall.'

Beth is silent, thinking about this fire coming out of the wall. She says to Rosalita: 'I was burned.'

'In the crash?'

'No. Not in the crash. The car never caught fire. I was burned by a man.'

Rosalita looks up at Beth. It is getting dark in the flat, but there is no electricity to turn on, so Rosalita lights a candle and sets it between them. By the light of this candle, whispering as if in church, Rosalita says: 'Your Mum tell me this one day. Your American man. Your Mum is crying. She says to me, Beth was going to have a beautiful life…'

'I did have a beautiful life. It ended early, that's all.'

Thaddeus lived in Kensington, when Kensington rents were cheap back then. He'd furnished his studio flat entirely from Habitat, down to the last teaspoon.

The carpet was rough cord. The bed was hard. On the hard bed, he took intimate photographs of Beth which he threatened to sell to *Penthouse* magazine. He said Bob Guccione was a friend of his and Guccione would gag for these. He said, 'Why waste your beauty, Beth? It'll be gone soon enough.'

Beth replied: 'I'm not wasting it. I'm giving it to you.'

And so he took it. He kept taking, taking, taking.

One night, as he was falling asleep, Beth said: 'I want to be with you for ever. Buy me a ring and marry me. Divorce Tricia. You don't love Tricia any more.'

'I don't love anyone any more,' he said.

These words sent a shock wave through Beth's heart. It began to beat very fast and she found it difficult to breathe.

'Why don't you?' she managed to say.

He got up and went to the window, staring out at the London night. 'You will see,' he said, 'when you're my age, when your life hasn't gone as you imagined…'

'See what?'

'I mean that you'll understand.'

She didn't understand, but she was always

careful, with Thaddeus, not to show ignorance or stupidity. He'd often said he thought American girls were smarter than English girls 'in important ways'. She tried to visualise the ring he would buy her: a diamond set high in a platinum claw.

Now, she thinks again about what he'd said – that his life hadn't *gone as he'd imagined*. And this leads her to wonder about the lives of her parents.

She knows she doesn't think of them as *having lives,* as such; they're just performing the duty of existence. They have dull, well-paid jobs, working for a Life Assurance company called Verity Life, with offices in Victoria Street, not far from the flat.

They pay for things. They watch television. The mother is half in love with Jack Lord, star of *Hawaii Five-O,* who drives a police motor launch at breathless speed. She loves it when a suspect is apprehended by Jack and he barks, 'Book him, Danno!' to his second-in-command. To the NUM hot-head, Arthur Scargill, defending the strike that has taken Britain into darkness, the mother often shouts, 'Book him, Danno!' And this always makes the father smile. The father's smile is like a weak gleam of sunlight falling upon the room.

The parents have survived all that Beth has done to them, all that has been done to her. Beth tells Rosalita that they will outlive their own daughter and this makes Rosalita bustle with agitation and reach for the crutches and tell her to get off the sofa and walk round the room. Beth tells her it's too painful to walk, but Rosalita has cradled in her arms matadors with lethal wounds; she's impatient with people complaining about pain. She gives the crutches to Beth and says, 'If you walk to the fireplace and back again, I will make hot chocolate with rum.' So Beth does as she is told and the pain makes her sweat.

The taste of the rum reminds her of being in Paris with Thaddeus.

She let herself get sacked from her job in the Gift Wrap counter in Harrods before they left, because part of her had decided they would never come back. They would live like Sartre and de Beauvoir on the Left Bank. Thaddeus would make a name for himself photographing French actors and models and objets d'art. They would drink black coffee at the Flore. She, Beth, would begin her career as a writer.

Thaddeus told her he'd been loaned an apartment 'with a great view' by an American friend. The view turned out to be of the Cimetière de Montparnasse, but Thaddeus continued to call it 'great' and liked to walk there, taking pictures of gravestones and mausoleums and artificial flowers, early in the morning. He said nothing about how long they would be staying in the City of Light.

The apartment had almost no furniture, as though the American friend hadn't yet decided to move in. The floors were wooden and dusty. The hot water boiler screamed when it was turned on.

Thaddeus and Beth slept on a mattress under a crocheted blanket of many colours.

Thaddeus said he had no money to buy sheets, but he had money, it seemed, to take them to an expensive gay and lesbian nightclub called *Elle et Lui*, where the personnel greeted him like a long-lost star and where a tall, beautiful woman called Fred became their friend and lover.

Fred lived in a hot little garret not far from their own empty, echoing apartment. Here, they drank rum and coke and made what Fred called *l'amour exceptionnel*. She said love between three people was *radioactive*; once you'd experienced it, it stayed in your blood for ever. She called Thaddeus 'Thad'. She whispered to Beth: 'Thad brought you here for this. It's the only kind of love he values because it's a democratic love. *Tu comprends?*'

She wanted to ask, does that mean what we had in London wasn't precious to him? But she didn't want to hear the answer. And she liked the way being touched by Fred excited Thaddeus. He called them 'the two most beautiful women in the world'.

'How long did you stay in Paris?' asks Rosalita.

Beth can't remember. Sometimes, she thinks it was a whole year and the seasons turned in the cemetery and the snow remoulded the tombs. Sometimes, she guesses that it was about a month or six weeks – until Thaddeus ran out of money.

She says to Rosalita: 'It was a kind of dream.'

She can't remember a summer season to the dream; only a cold spring arriving and the great grey *allées* of horse chestnut trees clothing themselves with green. There used to be a sequence of photographs of her, leaning out over the churning river in that same springtime, with her hair cut short like Jean Seberg, but these have been put away somewhere and their hiding place forgotten.

She can remember being ill for a while with *la grippe*. Fred came round, bringing an old fur coat, and covered her with this. Then Thad and Fred stood at the window, silhouetted against the wan light of day, and Beth could see them thinking, what is to be done now? – as though all human activity had come to a sudden end. And she knew that they would soon arouse each other by deft, secretive means and ask her to watch whatever they decided to do next. But she closed her eyes and breathed in the scent of mothballs on the fur and knew that she was drifting far away on a tide of naphthalene. She tells Rosalita: 'I can remember that feeling of floating out of my life, while fellatio was taking place.' And Rosalita crosses herself and whispers: 'Such things you have seen. Try to forget them now.'

She wants to forget them, but she can't. She says to Rosalita, 'Tell me something else about Setubal and the matadors.'

Rosalita replies that she should really get on and clean the bathroom, but then she goes to her bag and takes out a photograph of a young man in a matador costume. It's a faded picture, but the weight of gold sequins on the shoulder pads still cast a spangled luminescence onto the soft skin of the young man's face.

'My brother,' says Rosalita quietly. Then she lights a cigarette and sighs and inhales and explains: 'In Portugal we don't kill the bulls. We say there is no need for this blood. The *cavaleiros* on horseback stab them with *bandarilhas* and the *forcados* tease them until they are still.'

'And then what happens?'

'Then the matadors must come and risk their lives against them. Instead of killing with a sword, they stab with one last *bandarilha*. But a bull does not know it is not going to be killed. It will try to wound the matador with its horns. And this is what happened.'

'To your brother? He was wounded.'

'Yes. Antonio. You see how beautiful he was. More beautiful than me. He died of his wounds. And I see my parents thinking, It should have been Rosalita who was taken from us, not Antonio. So this is when I left Portugal and came to England.'

Beth is silent. She reaches out and holds Rosalita's hand.

Thaddeus and Beth came back from Paris. Perhaps it was summer by then, or autumn. Seasons are of no account in the way Beth remembers what happens next. It just happened in time, somewhere, and altered everything.

She became pregnant. She knew she would have to move out of her parent's flat; her father wouldn't tolerate her presence any more, once he knew her story.

While he and her mother were at work, she packed two suitcases with everything she owned, which came down to very little, just a few nice clothes, including a grey sleeveless dress from Mary Quant and four pairs of high-heeled boots. Pressed in among these things was the notebook she'd taken to Paris, which was meant to be full of notes towards a novel, but which contained no notes at all, only ink drawings of Thaddeus and Fred and of the dilapidated bedroom window, beyond which strange creatures floated in the Parisian sky: winged lambs, feathered serpents.

There were a few other things. A copy of *Le Petit Prince* by Saint-Exupéry and Tolstoy's *Anna Karenina*. There was a wooden tennis racket and two silver cups she'd won at school – one for being tennis champion, the other for 'good citizenship'. She would have left these behind but for the sentimental idea that she might one day show them to her child and the child might laugh and be proud.

She got into a taxi and arrived at Thaddeus's apartment towards the end of morning. She'd long ago asked to have her own key, but Thaddeus had said, 'Oh no. I never do this.' He had a way of making his utterances absolute and incontrovertible, like the authority of the CIA was behind them.

She got out of the taxi and rang the bell. Arriving at this door always made her heart lift, as though she was coming home to the only place which sheltered her. She set the suitcases down beside her, like two arthritic dogs who found movement difficult.

A stranger answered the door. Or rather somebody who was not quite a stranger, a French architect whom they had met once for lunch in Paris at the Dôme in Montparnasse. His name was Pierre.

Pierre said in his accented English: 'Thad said you would come. The flat belongs to me now.'

'What?' said Beth.

'Yes. I 'ave taken it on. Thad has gone back to California. I am sorry. May I offer you some tea?'

Beth says to Rosalita, 'I died there. Right there, between the two suitcases. That's when the real Beth died.'

Rosalita is sympathetic and yet sceptical. She says, 'I have seen many deaths, including Antonio's, and you have seen none. Death is not like that.'

'You don't understand, Rosalita,' says Beth. 'There was the girl who was loved by Thaddeus and when he left for California, that girl ceased to be.'

'But you are here. You are alive.'

'This 'I' is not that 'I'. It's the person who took over from her. It's the person who wrote the bestselling book called *The American Lover.*'

2.

The book was begun the day after the abortion.

The first scene was set in the abortionist's house (or 'clinic' as the surgeon called it) in Stanmore. It had a panelled hall and a view of a semi-rural recreation area.

Beth (or 'Jean' as she named her protagonist) was given an injection which she was told would make her forget everything that was going to happen. But the one thing she could remember was her inability to stop crying, and a nurse came and slapped her face, to make her stop, and afterwards there was a mark on her cheek where the slap had landed. The mark became a bruise and the bruise took a long time to fade.

Then, Beth's unborn baby was gone. She was a new self, who had no baby and no lover. Her bones felt as brittle and empty as cuttlefish shells and her head as heavy as a heap of wet earth and stones. It was difficult to make this wet earth function as a brain. It needed some skilled potter's hand to do it, but no such person was nearby.

Beth had a friend called Edwina, whom she'd known since schooldays, and thanks to Edwina – a girl with very clear skin, untouched by life – who drove her to Stanmore and collected her again, she was able to hide the abortion from the parents. They thought she and Edwina had gone on a boating picnic that day with some friends in

Henley. She told them she'd got the bruise on her face by being accidentally hit by an oar.

On the way back from Stanmore, Edwina asked Beth what she was going to do now. Beth felt sleepy and sick and didn't want to have to answer questions. She stared out at the night folding in on the long and terrible day. She said: 'I'm going to become Jean.'

'Who's Jean?' asked Edwina.

'A kind of heroine, except there's nothing heroic about her. I'm going to write her story and then try to sell it to a publisher.'

'Do you know anybody in the publishing world?' asked Edwina.

'No,' said Beth.

The abortion 'scene' began the story, but wasn't its beginning. It wasn't even its ending, because Beth had no idea what the ending would be, or even if there would *be* a proper ending, or whether the narrative wouldn't just collapse in upon itself without resolution.

What mattered was writing it: the act of words.

Beth began it in her Paris notebook. She let the words travel over the faces and bodies of Thad and Fred and over the window frame and the winged lambs beyond. To write about the abortion, about Thaddeus's desertion wasn't difficult; what was difficult was writing about the happiness that had come before. But she knew she had to do it somehow. You couldn't ask readers to care about the loss of something unless you showed them what that something had been.

The story began in London, then moved to Rome instead of Paris. Jean and her American lover, Bradley, were loaned an apartment just outside the Vatican City. Their transgressive love with a third person, Michaela, took place within two blocks of one of the holiest places on earth. The ringing of St Peter's bells tolled upon their ecstasy. In the apartment below them lived a lowly priest, whose life became a torment. Beth worked hard upon the sexual agonies he suffered. She wanted everything about the book to be shocking and new.

Beth wrote every day. She thought her parents would nag her to find a job to replace her old one at the Harrods Gift Wrap counter, but they didn't. It seemed that if you were a writer, you could get away with doing nothing else. Other people would go out to work and come back and you would still be there, unmoving in your chair, and they would make your supper and wash it up and you would collapse onto the sofa to watch Juke Box Jury. They would place forgiving goodnight kisses on your agitated head.

The father sometimes asked questions about the book, but all Beth would say was, 'You're probably going to hate it. It's about a girl going crazy. It's about things you don't talk about at Verity Life.'

But this didn't seem to make him anxious. It made him smile a tolerant smile, as though he thought Beth had underestimated him. And one Saturday morning, he took Beth to a second-hand shop off Tottenham Court Road and helped her choose a typewriter, and paid for it in cash. It was an old industrial Adler with a body made of iron and a pleasing Pica typeface and a delicate bell that tinkled when the carriage reached the end of a line. After Beth set the Adler on her desk, she felt less alone.

A letter came from California.

Thaddeus had that childish, loopy writing many Americans seemed to think was adequate to a grown-up life and his powers of self-expression were weak.

When Beth saw that the letter began *Dear Beth*, she laid it aside for a while, knowing it was going to smite her with its indifference.

Later, she took it up again and read: *I tried to tell you several times that I couldn't promise to stick around in London but I think you weren't listening. When you are my age, you will see. Money is important. I have to be a man of the world as well as a lover. Tricia has inherited her mother's house in Santa Monica. It's a nice beach-house, which I could never on my own afford. You would like it. And I can bathe in the ocean most days and forget about the cold of Europe. You will be OK. If you go to Paris, see Fred and tell her the Old American has gone back to the sun. Love, Thad.*

Beth folded the letter into her notebook and went and lay down on her bed. She thought about the crocheted blanket that had covered them in Paris: the rich smell of it which was both beautiful and tainted. She thought about the lens of Thaddeus's camera pointed at her body and the shutter opening and closing, opening and closing, gathering her further and further into a prison from which there was no exit.

There was only the book.

It was written in eleven weeks. Everything that Beth had experienced with Thaddeus was relived through Jean and Bradley. The slow, exquisite way a single orgasm was achieved sometimes took a page to describe. Fred/Michaela became a male-to-female transsexual with handsome white breasts. Bradley became a painter. His own genitals, both aroused and dormant, featured repetitively in his art. Jean was a beauty, with a mouth men tried to kiss in the street and tumbled blonde hair. She was Desire Absolute. Bradley and Michaela screamed and wept over her and sometimes lost all control and beat the floor, while the poor priest lay in his narrow bed beneath them and jabbered his Hail Marys as a penance for his own sexual incontinence.

It was typed out on the Adler, with a blotchy blue carbon copy underneath. Beth stared at this carbon copy. She thought, Jean is the smart top-copy of a person now, and I'm the carbon, messed up and fragile and half invisible. But she also understood that no book quite like this had ever been written by a twenty-year-old girl. The pages crackled with radioactive heat. Readers could be contaminated in their thousands – or in their millions.

Beth now remembered that she knew nobody in the publishing world. She'd had no idea it was a 'world', exactly. She'd imagined there were just writers and printers and the people who paid them doing some slow gavotte together, which nobody else ever saw. All she could do was buy the *Writers' and Artists' Year Book* from Smith's, choose an agent from its pages who promised 'international representation' and send off the book.

Rosalita sometimes says how sad it is that most of what she and Beth talk about in the winter afternoons is concerned with endings of one kind or another. But she likes the next bit of Beth's story. What happened next seemed to promise new happiness: Beth was taken on by an agent.

'The agent was called Beatrice,' Beth tells her. 'After she'd read the book, she invited me round to her office in Canonbury Square. There was a bottle of champagne waiting. She said, "I can sell this novel in forty countries."'

'Forty countries!' gasps Rosalita. 'In Portugal, we probably couldn't name more than half of those.'

'Well,' says Beth, 'I probably couldn't either. I never knew Panama was a country, I thought it was a canal. And I've forgotten the list of all the places where the book was sold. All I know is that money started to come to me – so much money I thought I would drown in it.'

'And then you buy the red car?' asks Rosalita.

'No. Not that car. That was a gift, which came later. I bought another car, a Maserati. But a car didn't seem much to own, so I bought a house in Kensington and then I drove to France with Beatrice and I bought a second house in St-Tropez.'

'Were you happy?' asks Rosalita.

'No. I was famous. I made the cover of *Paris Match* and *Time Magazine*. I perfected the way I looked. Not like I look now, Rosalita. It was my moment of being beautiful. I got letters from all over the world from people wanting to go to bed with me. I probably could have slept with Jean-Paul Belmondo and Marcello Mastroianni, if I'd tried.'

'Ah, Mastroianni. What a god!'

'Yes, he was, I suppose,' says Beth. 'But I never met him.'

As if to affirm the disappointment of not meeting Mastroianni, the lights in the flat go out suddenly and the afternoon dark presses in. Rosalita goes hunting for candles, but can't find any, so she lights the gas fire and by its scented blue light changes the subject to ask Beth what her mother and father thought about the book.

'Oh,' says Beth. 'Well, I remember the way

they looked at me. Sorrow and pity. No pride. They told me I'd sold my soul.'

'And what did you say?'

'I said no, I gave my soul away for nothing. Thaddeus still has it. He keeps it somewhere, in a drawer, with old restaurant bills and crumbs of stale tobacco and discarded polaroids that have faded to the palest *eau-de-nil* green.'

Rosalita doesn't know what to say to this. Perhaps she doesn't understand it? Her comprehension of English is known to falter now and then. The gas fire flickers and pops. Rosalita gets up and puts on her coat and before leaving places a kiss on Beth's unwashed hair.

After *The American Lover,* there would need to be another book, a follow-up, so Beatrice said. Did Beth want the world to think she was a one-book wonder?

Beth replied that she didn't care what the world thought. She was rich and she was going to live. She was going to live so fast, there would be no moment in any part of the day or night to remember Thaddeus. She would crush him under the weight of her new existence.

She went to St-Tropez, to redesign the garden of her house. She drank most nights until she passed out and slept sometimes with a beach lifeguard called Jo-Jo, who liked to stare at pornographic magazines in the small hours.

The garden progressed. In a shaded area of

Corsican pines, Beth built a temple, which she filled with an enormous day-bed, hung with soft white linen. She spent a long time lying on this day-bed alone, drinking, smoking, watching the the sea breezes take the pines unaware. News came from Beatrice that *The American Lover* had been sold in five more countries. A Swedish director wanted to turn it into a film. An Icelandic composer was writing *The 'American Lover' Symphony.* Pirated copies had reached The Soviet Union and a young Russian writer called Vassily wrote to say he was writing a sequel to the novel, in which Bradley would be executed by a KGB agent in Volgograd. *This,* he wrote, *will be a very violent death, very terrible, very fitting to this bad man, and I, Vassily will smuggle this decadent book out of Russia to the USA and it will become as famous as your book and I will be rich and live in Las Vegas.*

In this cold, dark winter of 1974, Beth spends more and more time looking at her press file. There is not one picture of Thaddeus in it. He is the missing third dimension in a two-dimensional world. Beth's vacant face, caught in the white glare of photographers' flashbulbs, looks more and more exhausted with the search for something that is always out of sight.

She can remember this: how she looked for Thaddeus in Iceland, in shabby, raucous nightclubs, in hotel dining rooms, in the crowd of tourists congregating at a hot spring. Later, she searched for him in Canada, on the cold foreshore of Lake

Ontario, in a brand new shopping mall, in the publisher's smart offices, on the precipice of Niagara Falls.

And then in New York, where, finally she went and was fêted like a movie star, she kept finding him. He was at a corner table in Sardi's. He was standing alone in the lobby of the Waldorf Astoria. He was in Greenwich village, walking a poodle. He was buying a silk scarf in Bloomingdale's. He was lying on a bench in Central Park. He was among the pack of photographers at her book launch.

She thinks that he came back to her so strongly there, in America, because of all the voices that sounded like his. And one evening, as she was crossing Lexington Avenue, she heard yet another of these voices and she stumbled and fell down, slayed by her yearning for him. The man she was with, a handsome gallery owner of Persian origin, assumed she was drunk (she *was* often drunk) and hurled her into the first cab he could flag down and never saw her again.

She sat in the back of the cab like a dead person, unable to move. The sound of the cab's engine reminded her of the motor launch Thaddeus had once hired on the Seine. The day had been so fine that Thaddeus had taken off his shirt and she had put her arms round his thin torso and stroked his chest hair. And the ordinariness of him, the way he tried so hard and did so much with this fragile, unremarkable frame of his had choked her with a feeling that was not quite admiration and not quite pity, but which bound her to him more strongly than she had ever been bound, as though her arms were bandages.

In the screeching New York night, Beth wondered whether, after all, after living so hard to forget him, she wouldn't fly to California and stand on the beach in front of his house at dawn, waiting until he got up and came to her.

She imagined that when he came to her, they would stand very still, holding onto one another and the sighing of the ocean would soothe them into believing that time had captured them in some strange, forgiving embrace.

When Beth came back from America, she got married. Her husband was an English aristocrat called Christopher. He was a semi-invalid with encroaching emphysema, but he was kind. He told her she needed someone to care for her, and she felt this to be true: she was being suffocated by the surfeits of her existence. Christopher said that, on his part, Beth would 'decorate' his life in ways he had often thought would be appropriate to it, but he reassured her that he preferred sex with men and would let her sleep alone. His house in Northamptonshire had a beautiful apple orchard, where he built her a wooden cabin. He suggested she might write her books in this cabin, and he furnished it with care.

She spent some time there, playing Bob Dylan songs, watching the apple blossom falling in the wind, but she knew she would never write another book. She had no life to put into it, only the half-life that she'd been leading, since writing *The American Lover.* And the years were beginning to pass. She was being forgotten. People knew that she was the author of what had come to be known as a 'great classic about transgressive first love' but times were changing, and they couldn't quite remember what all the fuss had been about.

Beth liked Christopher because he sheltered her. When her house in St-Tropez burned down, Christopher began on her behalf a long wrangle with a French insurance firm. But he couldn't win it. The house had been struck by lightning, so the insurers said, and nobody could be insured against 'acts of God'.

Christopher lamented all the money Beth had poured into this house, but she found that she didn't really care about it – either about the house or about the money. The person who got mad was Beatrice. She screamed at Beth that she was letting everything slip through her fingers. 'You will soon see,' she said, 'that the money will dry up, and then what are you going to do?'

She didn't know or care. With Christopher, she had suddenly entered upon a period of quiet. It was as if her heart had slowed. She liked to work in the greenhouses with Christopher's gardeners (one of whom, a handsome youth called Matty, was his most favoured lover), potting up seedlings, tending strawberries, nurturing herbs. Only now and again did some resistance to this quiet life rise up within her. Then she would get into the new red E-type Jaguar that Christopher had given her and drive at terrible speed down the Northamptonshire lanes, screaming at the sky.

'Were you trying to die?' Rosalita asks her.

'Not trying,' Beth replies. 'Just laying a bet.'

'And you didn't think, maybe you hurt or kill someone else?'

'No. I didn't think.'

'This is not good,' says Rosalita. 'You were like the bull which wounded my brother. You had a small brain.'

One time, she just went on driving until she got to London. She called Christopher to say that she was safe and then stayed in her Kensington house, doing nothing but drink. Her wine cellar was emptying but there were still a few cases of champagne left, so she drank champagne.

She'd intended to drive back to Northamptonshire the following day, but she didn't. She was glad to find herself in a city. She found that if she went to bed drunk, Thaddeus would often visit her in her dreams. He would come into her room very quietly and say, 'Hey, kid.' He would remove the hat that he sometimes wore and sit on the bed and stroke her hand. This was as far as the dreams ever got, and Beth began to work out that this affectionate, silent figure was waiting for something. He would never say what. He sat very still. Beth could smell his aftershave and hear his quiet breathing.

Then, one morning, she believed she understood. Thaddeus was asking for her forgiveness.

★

She typed out a letter on the old Adler. She felt very calm, almost happy.

She told Thaddeus that she'd been crazy with grief and this grief and its craziness just wouldn't let her alone. She said: *I guess the book said it all, if you read the book. Jean loves Bradley way too much and when he leaves her, she's destroyed. I let Jean die, but I'm alive (in certain ways, anyway) and I have a husband with a very English sort of kind heart.*

But when it came to typing the word 'forgive' Beth faltered. Though in her dream, Thaddeus had been affectionate and quiet, Beth now thought that he would find the whole idea of 'forgiveness' sentimental. She could hear him say: 'You're way off, *ma pute,* way off! We had a few turns on the merry-go-round, or whatever the British call that little musical box thing that takes you round in a circle. And then one of us got off. That's all that happened. There was no crime.'

Beth tore the letter out of the Adler and

threw it away. She opened another bottle of champagne, but found the taste of it bitter. She asked herself what was left to her by way of any consolation, if forgiveness was going to be refused.

'After that,' she tells Rosalita, 'I gave up on things. I drove back to Christopher. His emphysema was beginning to get very bad. I stayed with him through his last illness until he died. I ran out of money. Christopher left his whole estate to Matty, his gardener friend, so I had to leave Northamptonshire. I missed the apple orchard and my little cabin there. The Kensington house was valuable, but it was all mortgaged by then. And after that there was the crash.'

'Tell me,' says Rosalita.

It's a winter afternoon, but the lights are still on. Rosalita is coiling up the Hoover cable.

'Well,' I'd hung onto that car. It seemed like the only thing that anyone had given to me and not taken away again. But I hadn't taken care of it. It was a heap of rust. People were right not to give me things, I guess. My brain wasn't big enough to take care of them.

'I wasn't trying to kill myself, or anything. I was driving to see my friend, Edwina, the one with the lovely skin, who'd helped me through the abortion.

I was on some B-road in Suffolk. I braked on a bend and the brakes locked and that's all I can remember. The car went half way up a tree. That long snout the E-type has, that was concertina'd and the concertina of metal smashed up my legs.'

'Right,' says Rosalita, putting the hoover away. 'Now you are going to do some walking, then we will have rum and hot chocolate.'

The Three Day Week has ended with the miners' defeat. Britain tries to get 'back to normal'.

'There is no normal,' says Beth to Rosalita. 'The only "normal" has been talking to you in the afternoons.'

But that is ending, just as everything else seems, always, to end. Rosalita is leaving London to return to Setubal, to nurse her dying mother.

'She doesn't deserve me,' Rosalita comments. 'She only loved Antonio, never me. But in my blood I feel I owe her this.'

'Don't go,' pleads Beth.

'Alas,' says Rosalita, 'it has to be like this. Some things just have to be.'

On Rosalita's last day both she and Beth feel unbearably sad. As Rosalita walks out of the flat for the last time, she says: 'All the secrets you told me I shall keep inside me, very safe.'

'And your brother, Antonio, the matador,' says Beth. 'I will keep his memory safe. I will think about the light on his face.'

Beth waits for the clunk of the elevator's arrival. Then she hears Rosalita get into the elevator and close the door and she remains very still, listening to the long sigh of the lift going down.

A year after Rosalita leaves, Beth is able to walk once more, with the aid of a stick.

One day she takes the bus to Harrods, suddenly interested to visit the place where she'd worked long ago, cutting wrapping paper with mathematical care, fashioning bows and rosettes out of ribbon, making the most insignificant of gifts look expensive and substantial. It had seemed to her a futile thing to be doing, but now it doesn't strike her as futile. She can see that a person's sanity might sometimes reside in the appreciation of small but aesthetically pleasing things.

Holding fast to her stick, she gets on to the familiar escalators. The feeling of being moved around so effortlessly, whether up or down, has always given her pleasure. As a child, she used to beg to be brought here, to the escalators. She loved to watch the people moving in the opposite direction, like dolls on a factory conveyor belt.

She's watching them now, these human dolls: a multitude of faces, ascending to Soft Furnishings, descending to Perfumerie and Banking, all locked away in their own stories.

Then she sees Thaddeus.

He's descending. She's going up. She stares at him as he passes, then cranes her head round to keep watching him as he goes on down. And she sees that he, too, has turned. Changed as she is, he has recognised her. His face is locked on hers.

She gets off the escalator at the first floor (Lingerie, Ladies Shoes, Children's Clothes). Her heart cries out for her to run to the descending escalator, to follow Thaddeus, to rush into his arms. But her body is too slow. Her legs won't let her run. She stands on the first floor landing, looking down.

She sees Thaddeus stop and look up. Then he joins the people surging towards the exit doors and follows them out.

The Authors

Tessa Hadley has written five novels including *Accidents in the Home* (2002), *The London Train* (2011) and *Clever Girl* (2013), and two collections of short stories: *Sunstroke* (2007) and *Married Love* (2012). She has had novels longlisted for the Guardian First Book Award, for the Orange Prize (twice), and for the Welsh Book of the Year (twice); *Sunstroke* was shortlisted for The Story Prize in the US, and *Married Love* was shortlisted for the Edge Hill Prize. She has twice had stories in The O. Henry Prize collection. She publishes stories regularly in the *New Yorker*, reviews for the *London Review of Books* and the *Guardian*, and is a Professor at Bath Spa University, teaching mostly on the MA in Creative Writing. She has also published a critical book on Henry James. Hadley was a judge for the BBC National Short Story Award in 2011. She was born in Bristol and lives in London.

Francesca Rhydderch has a degree in Modern Languages from Newnham College, Cambridge, and a PhD in English from Aberystwyth University. She attended her first creative writing course, led by BBC Executive Producer Kate McAll and novelist Patricia Duncker, as the recipient of a BBC/Ty Newydd bursary in 2010. Her début novel, *The Rice Paper Diaries*, published in 2013, was longlisted for the Authors' Club Best First Novel Award and won the Wales Book of the Year Award 2014 for Fiction. Rhydderch's short stories have been published in magazines and anthologies and broadcast on Radio 4. She recently received a Literature Wales bursary to work on her first collection of short fiction. Other projects include a play in Welsh, 'Cyfaill', about iconic Welsh-language writer Kate Roberts, for which she was shortlisted for the Theatre Critics Wales Best Playwright Award 2014. Rhydderch was born in Aberystwyth and now lives in Cardiff.

Lionel Shriver is an American writer who lives in London. The author of 11 novels, she is best known for the *New York Times* bestsellers *So Much for That* (a finalist for the 2010 National Book Award and the Wellcome Trust Book Prize) and *The Post-Birthday World* (*Entertainment Weekly*'s Book of the Year and one of *Time*'s top ten for 2007), as well as the international bestseller *We Need to Talk About Kevin*. The 2005 Orange Prize winner, *Kevin* passed the million-copies-sold mark several years ago, and was adapted for an award-winning feature film by Lynne Ramsay in 2011. Both *Kevin* and *So Much for That* have been dramatised for BBC Radio 4. Currently a columnist for *Standpoint*, she is a widely published journalist who writes for the *Guardian*, the *New York Times*, the *Sunday Times*, the *Financial Times*, and the *Wall Street Journal*, among many other publications. Her eleventh novel, *Big Brother*, was published in spring of 2013. Shriver has been shortlisted twice previously for the BBC National Short Story Award in 2009 and 2013.

Zadie Smith was born in north-west London in 1975 and now lives in New York. She is the author of the novels *NW*, *White Teeth*, *The Autograph Man* and *On Beauty*; a collection of essays, *Changing My Mind*; and a short story called 'The Embassy of Cambodia'. She is also the editor of *The Book of Other People*. *White Teeth* was the winner of the 2000 Guardian First Book Award, the 2000 Whitbread First Novel Award, the 2000 James Tait Black Memorial Prize and a Betty Trask award, and was shortlisted for the Orange Prize 2001. *On Beauty* was shortlisted for the Man Booker Prize in 2005 and won the Orange Prize in 2006. *NW* was shortlisted for the Women's Prize for Fiction in 2013.

Rose Tremain's bestselling novels have won many awards, including the Orange Prize (*The Road Home*), the Whitbread Novel of the Year (*Music & Silence*), the James Tait Black Memorial Prize and the Prix Femina Etranger (*Sacred Country*). *Restoration* was shortlisted for the Booker Prize in 1989 and made into a film in 1995. The sequel, *Merivel*, was published to rapturous acclaim in

2012, and *The Telegraph* described the character of Robert Merivel as 'one of the great imaginative creations in English literature of the past fifty years'. Tremain was made a CBE in 2007 and was appointed Chancellor of the University of East Anglia in 2013. She lives in Norfolk and London with the biographer, Richard Holmes. Tremain has been shortlisted once before for the BBC National Short Story Award in 2006.

About The BBC National Short Story Award

The BBC National Short Story Award in partnership with Booktrust is one of the most prestigious for a single short story and celebrates the best in home-grown short fiction. The ambition of the Award, which is now in its ninth year, is to expand opportunities for British writers, readers and publishers of the short story. The winning author receives £15,000, the runner-up £3,000 and the three further shortlisted authors £500 each. All five shortlisted stories are broadcast on BBC Radio 4.

The previous winners are: Sarah Hall (2013), Miroslav Penkov (in 2012, when the Award accepted international entries to commemorate the Olympics); D.W. Wilson (2011); David Constantine (2010); Kate Clanchy (2009); Clare Wigfall (2008); Julian Gough (2007) and James Lasdun (2006).

Award Partners:

BBC Radio 4 is the world's biggest single commissioner of short stories. Short stories are broadcast every week attracting more than a million listeners. **www.bbc.co.uk/radio4**

Booktrust is an independent charity that changes lives through reading. Booktrust is responsible for a number of successful national reading promotions, sponsored book prizes and creative reading projects aimed at encouraging readers to discover and enjoy books. **www.booktrust.org.uk**

More on: **www.booktrust.org.uk/bbcnssa**
Follow us on Twitter: @Booktrust #BBCNSSA